The Mouse in the Moon

A Collection of Children's Poems

Raymond Copp

Copyright 2016

To Loren

He who forms the mountains, creates the wind, and reveals his thoughts to man, he who turns dawn to darkness, and treads the high places of the earth — the LORD God Almighty is his name — Amos 4:13

First published by Dog Ear Publishing
4011 Vincennes Rd
Indianapolis, IN 46268
www.dogearpublishing.net

ISBN: 978-1-4575-5402-5

This book is printed on acid-free paper.

Printed in the United States of America

Table of Contents

The Mouse in the Moon

I remember that night
near the end of July
when I lay in my bed
staring up at the sky

And spotted a wonder
high over my house—
On the moon overhead
was the face of a MOUSE!

How did he get there
that mouse in the moon?
Did he blast into space
with a mighty VAROOM?
Did he ride on a trolley
or hot air balloon?
I'm in love (so in love)
with the mouse in the moon

When did he get there
that mouse in the moon?
Did he go after breakfast
or mid-afternoon?
Did he travel at midnight
with a witch on a broom?
I'm in love (so in love)
with the mouse in the moon.

Just why *did* he go there
that mouse in the moon?
To escape from a cat
that invaded his room?
Or conquer a land
in the name of the king
or just for the pleasure
of one more new thing?

It took me a month
just to figure it out—
The reason he skittered
and scampered about

The reason he tumbled
like on a trapeze
It wasn't for fun—
He did it for CHEESE!

You see it's a fact
(almost everyone knows)
a mouse doesn't read
or wear any clothes—
He can't play a trumpet
or use water skis
but he'd go to the moon
for a big piece of CHEESE!

I've never learned how
the mouse traveled in space
or when he had settled
alone in that place

But I knew *why* he stayed
as I watched from my room—
I'm in love (so in love)
with the mouse in the moon

Alberta LaChoo

Far to the north in a land of snow
Deep in the woods where the real men go
Bravin' the ice and frozen bog
Choppin' up trees n' haulin' out logs

In the lumber town of Wishie Waloo
Was a loggin' train Alberta LaChoo

Loadin' up timber on her flatbed cars
Lashin' 'em tight with chains n' bars
Blowin' her whistle to clear the way
Alberta girl's a haulin' a load today

Clickedly-clack and tickety-tack
Cold wheels singin' on the railroad track
Sweatin' up grades, pullin' on the flat
Coastin' on corners to the sidin' track

Lumbermen waitin' for a ride to town
Sweat soaked bodies gotta' lay 'em down
Bugs in their pockets, twigs in their hair
Dirt in their socks and their underwear

Worst of the lot was Frenchy Balou
Outlaw varmint n' scourge of the crew
His talk was rough and breath was worse
He had no manners and loved to curse

Chewed on nails, splittin' out the ends
Had no schoolin' and had no friends
Drooled when he ate, bugs on his shirt
Covered with lice n' fleas n' dirt

Lumberjack work is hard they say
Breakin' your back from dawn each day
Livin' in the woods, campin' in the cold
Dangers so many ya' never get old

Such was the bunch that stood by the side
Waitin' for the train to give 'em a ride

Shaggy varmints they looked insane
Itchin' fer trouble they boarded that train
Frenchy Balou was the first in line—
First you could say in a line of swine

But when that pirate found his place
A friendly look came over his face
He called to the train Alberta LaChoo
"Hello Alberta, how do you do!"

"Hello Francois," Alberta smiled
"I'm glad you boys are not so wild
A lady like me needs more in a man
Than bulky muscles and a sun-baked tan"

"A lady wants manners and grand finesse
Good discussion and handsome dress
So wash your hands and scrub your face
Take your seats and find your place
There's the whistle, it's time to dine—
We've just reserved the finest wine"

The change in them would startle you
To see such gents as Frenchy Balou
Sittin' in their seats sippin' on tea
Holding their cups so daintily

Making such talk as fit for a king
Or duke or earl or some such thing

They spoke of weather in the south of
France
The cut of trousers and length of pants
A game of Cricket and a greyhound race
The latest fashion from place to place

They dined on rabbit and roasted quail
Veal scaloppini and lobster tail
Warm plum pudding and peach flambé
Then topped it off with French café

Alberta LaChoo had pulled that train
Of backwoods gentry through the rain
Down to the valley and the town below
Down to the camp where the woodsmen go

Into the station she stopped on the track
Opened the door and called to the back
"All right boys, we've reached the camp
It's dark outside so take a lamp
Then walk on home and go to bed"
As each got off, they turned and said—

"Good night, Alberta, do sleep well"
But as they left they began to smell

And laugh and burp and spit and curse
Each one acting out his worst
Bugs in their pockets, fleas in their hair
Dirt in their socks and their underwear

Alberta sighed and let off some steam
Her boiler cooled she began to dream
Of fancy parties and royal balls
Of moonlit walks and starlit halls
Of friendly words and a lover's kiss
Of all the things she had to miss

But if you stand one day by the track
As the frigid cold climbs up your back
You'll see a train parked on the side—
With loggers waitin' for chance to ride

The smoky old engine went clackity-clack
as it hustled, exhausted, and clung to the track.
Though once she was called "Queen of the Line"
and carried fine people from Chester to Rhine–
She now barely struggled along down the line,
and bore the sad title of "Old Number Nine."

Engineer of the train was Walter McBride,
a jovial sort from the Town of New Hyde.
And though she was rusty and bumpy to ride,
"Old Nine" trudged along with rails as a guide.

It's lonely at night on the rails of our land,
where noone at all would lend a kind hand,
to an engine who tried, but just couldn't go–
not fastest of fast, but slowest of slow.

But Walter was there, to stack up the wood
and whisper a word to make her feel good.

"Old Nine" might have quit, just give up the jig–
If it hadn't have been for her love of that pig!

Charles was a pig, and a strange one at that,
who wore an old jacket and red feathered hat.
He lived on a farm near Shady Tree Glade
just where the train would slow for the grade.

He'd wait near the bridge on Sassafras Creek,
near where "Old Nine" had slowed to a creep.
Then Walter would grab that pig by the hoof–
and swing him on board right onto the roof!

You've probably not seen a pig on a train,
sitting on top in the snow and the rain.
A smile on his face and snow on his snout,
the wind blowing jacket and feathers about.

And just as "Old Nine" started up from the flats
with the pig on the roof in his jacket and hat,
she'd signal the tunnel by whistle toots three–
and Charles would oink and holler WHOOPEE!

Then on the way back, near Shady Tree Glade
where "Old Number Nine" slowed again for the grade.
Charles would jump off near Sassafras Creek,
and set off for home with soot on his feet.

Until on a night, when Charles took a seat,
near the grade, near the bridge on Sassafras Creek.
To wait for the whistle to sound in the flats,
and straighten his jacket and red feathered hat.
He waited and waited, with no train in sight,
And worried and fretted far into the night.
Until the day broke, then sun finally shone,
and Charles the pig walked slowly on home.

And never again did "Old Nine" repeat
her run down the line near Sassafras Creek.
Parked in the yard and salvaged for parts,
they took out her boiler, but never her heart.

And never again did the pig ride a train,
sitting on top in the snow and the rain.
But if you go at night, way out on the line–
and listen in quiet from Chester to Rhine.
You may hear a whistle, faint as can be–
and the oink of a pig as he hollers WHOOPEE!

All the Pretty Animals

Master of Creation,
Earth and land and sea
All the pretty animals
Made for you and me

Like Richelieu Rhinoceros
And Glenda Kangaroo
Piccadilly Platypus
Abercrombie Shrew

Slippery Salamanders
Swarming buzzing bees
Crocodiles and Lady Bugs
Monkeys in the trees

Calamity Koala Bear
Manitoba Goose
Lydia the Elephant
Lemmings on the loose

God of all Creation
Wind and rain and air
Maker of the Universe—
With an artist's flair!

Baxter Duck

In the spring
there's a thing
that robins sing
and bluebells ring

If you're a mouse
or feathered grouse
just ask your spouse
to clean the house

If he gets stuck
runs out of luck
has too much muck
Call Baxter Duck

The duck is sure
and mature
an epicure
of furniture

If your home
is in Nome
or in Rome
with a dome

Baxter's smart
He won't start
to clean a part
without a cart

So when you're stuck
Baxter Duck
has the pluck
To clean your muck!

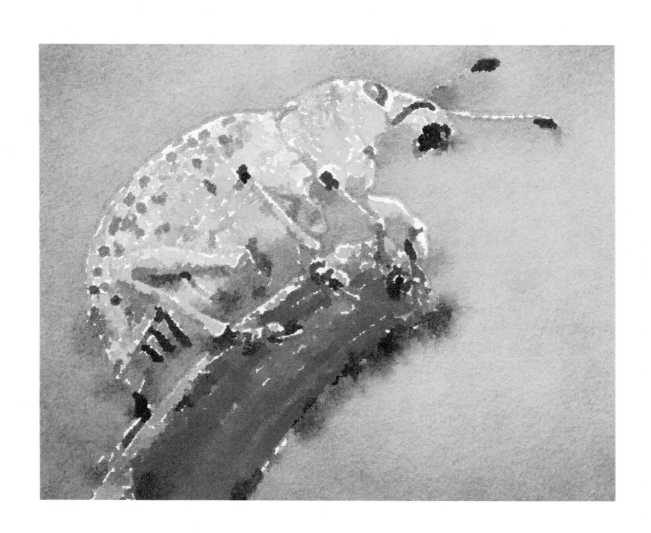

Big-Wig Bug

Under a cover of soft garden green
The City of Bugville nestles unseen
An insect city of largest size
Of reputation spread far and wide

Bugville bugs are handsomely paid
Working mostly in building and trade
Bees selling pollen for homemade honey
Ants building houses for jelly-bean money

The mayor of Bugville was a lug of a bug
A terrible brute and mostly a thug
Ruling the insects in horrible ways
Like beating them up when going astray

Big-wig Bug (he thought himself great),
A "Beetle of Power and "Bug Head-of-State"
He spent his time making rules and orders
For insects and bugs within Bugville borders.

He had not a friend (or an ally) it's true
Why he would want one he hadn't a clue
He didn't need chums, he thought rather smugly
Beetles were handsome, but friends were so ugly!

Insects paid taxes which he spent on candy
To eat for his breakfast and dinner when handy
Until one sad day when the candy ran low
He ran to the garden where carrots did grow

Bring me more candy! (He had quite a habit)
He yelled to a bird and then to a rabbit
But Bunny was crunching beets by the bunch
And Bird simply ate Big Wig for his lunch!

Under the cover of soft garden shade
The City of Bugville engages in trade
But insects are smiling; frowns are so rare
The City of Bugville needs a new Mayor!

Dream for a Nation:

Broken Apple
and the Ghost Dancers

Before settlers came to Iroquois Soto
and snow covered the wilderness forest
Broken Apple lived among the Cho-Sasné
whose people had built great birch lodges
along the banks of the Onondaga River
nestled at the foot of Ghost Mountain–
Like a child nestled in his father's arms

As the youngest son of Running Feather
Broken Apple lived in the medicine lodge
and listened quietly at council meetings
to elders speak of bleak winters to come
and of white settlers moving to Iroquois Soto

Running Feather, some said, got strong medicine
and great power from spirits of the next life
who would often visit upon him grand visions
and dream-messages from warriors long since gone
or unearthly prophecy from those not yet born
Broken Apple, as Running Feather's little son
was destined to have a spirit vision too–
and deliver an unsettling warning to his people

It was customary for young boys, like Broken Apple
to remain alone on the father of mountains
where, according to tribal legend, spirit warriors
would come and bring counsel from the next life
And, through a vision, reveal events yet to come

Ghost Mountain looked cold and foreboding
with snow capped peaks and windswept slopes
when Broken Apple, like his father before him
found a cave and sat before the dream-fire
to await spirit visitors from the great beyond

As the fire blazed, prancing shadows took ghostly form
and Broken Apple watched in amazement as shadows
transformed into spirit warriors clad in deerskin pants
their long hair tied by the red band of brotherhood
worn only by the wisest and bravest of his people

Mystic spirit warriors danced in the shadowy light
and chanted age-old war songs of the ancestors
until unseen drums stopped their fearful music—
The dream-cave assumed an eerie, unearthly quiet
and ghost dancers sat by the fire with Broken Apple
with the blood-red paint of war on their faces
and red-feathered war arrows in their quivers

The spirit warriors did not speak to Broken Apple
but talked among themselves as if he wasn't there
As they spoke, Broken Apple watched their words
played out as visions upon the cave walls
Spectral images of a time the boy did not know

Broken Apple saw great trees pulled by their roots
and laid side-by-side as far as the eagle flies
and over these trees rode a long string of ponies
each with its bridle tied to the one in front
and the first pony was the largest and strongest
and breathed fire and smoke from its nose and ears

The boy saw deer and bear and other animals
run wildly away as the ponies drew closer
He saw brave warriors shoot arrows at the ponies
but they galloped on and could not be stopped

Broken Apple saw many people of different colors
wearing outlandish costumes move into the valley
and build strange lodges taller than great spruces
and he wondered where his own people had gone
for they did not seem to live among the strangers

The medicine-boy woke to find the spirits gone
with only fading shadows dancing in the cave
He was puzzled by the dream-message
and could not understand its meaning

Elders were gathered in the medicine lodge
when Broken Apple stepped through the door
and stood small and timid before them
The elders were amazed by Broken Apple
for the boy of seven winters still wore
the blood-red paint of war on his face
and carried a quiver of red-feathered arrows

Broken Apple told of warrior ghost dancers
and of visions played out upon the cave walls
and a long string of war ponies breathing fire
and the tall lodges of people of different colors
and the riddle of where his own people had gone

He stood anxiously before the tribal council
expecting the celebration which usually followed
a medicine-boy's return from Ghost Mountain—
But there was no merrymaking, or even laughter
The elders said nothing to little Broken Apple
but instead gazed fixedly at the council fire

Then Running feather embraced his weary son
and wiping blood-red war paint from his face
laid Broken Apple gently onto his own bed

For in the stillness of the medicine lodge
as elders sat haunted by the dream-message
a father covered his son with warm bearskins
and Broken Apple, innocent little prophet
drifted off to an ancient land of dreams
as the melodic whistle of a locomotive
drifted menacingly through the valley below

Butternut Mole

Persuaded by nature soon after his birth
Butternut Mole dug under the earth
Tunneling deeper not making a sound
Quietly! Quietly! Under the ground

Under the soil he spent all his time
No wonder his nose was layered with grime
No candle or flashlight to brighten his way
Butternut tunneled through mountains of clay

An ambitious sort (an expert at mining)
Butternut craved the most curious dining
Mud on his ears; dirt clung to his tummy
Whatever he craved, it sure must be yummy!

Butternut's whiskers were dirty and icky
Brown goo on his fur made him so sticky
Kinfolk were baffled by Butternut's hue
Was this some special unusual glue?

He turned up his nose at beetles and grubs
His stomach would sour when sniffing a bug
Butternut longed for a snack like no other
He nurtured a craving for thick peanut butter!

He ate it for breakfast (he loved it for dinner)
Butternut Mole grew fatter not thinner
Worm pie was slimy (he just couldn't try it)
So Butternut Mole was put on a diet!

Butternut Mole lived under the earth
Just as he did since the day of his birth
Tunneling deeper not making a sound
Quietly! Quietly! Under the ground

Mee Furew

About a zillion years ago
when all the world was new
A kid like me lived by the sea –
His name was Mee Furew

Shaggy coat of Mammoth fur
hung loosely on his back–
Shoes of Crocosaurus hide
with speckles red and black

Furews all lived together
in caverns made of stone–
Nestled snug in seaside cliffs
their cool suburban homes

Furniture of finest rock
beds of softest hide
Ocean breeze cool at night
Furews tucked safe inside

Families dined on lizard eggs
Froglodites and hares–
Mammoth soup, snakeosaurs
And shaggy dino-bears

Mee looked for a better way
to get from here to there
Than on his bike he didn't like
with wheels of stony squares

He grabbed a rock, began to knock
stone pieces to the ground
Soon Mee had chiseled rocky wheels
made not square– but round

Was Mee like me? I asked myself–
Were Mee and I the same?
And realized to my surprise
We shared a common name

So when I think I'm different
from Mee who lived before–
I see the Mee beside the sea
and wonder all the more

cedric's big day

cedric inched along the ground
minding his affairs–
suddenly a human hand
raised him in the air

"oh, mommy look! a pat-e-killer
can i take him home?"
it's caterpillar, wendy dear–
just leave him there alone!"

wendy did take cedric home
and put him in a jar
to wait and see the butterfly
become a fashion star

cedric built a grand cocoon
attached it to a twig
made himself at home inside–
it certainly was big!

wendy checked it every day
knew cedric was inside
magically transforming
to a gorgeous butterfly

cedric sensed the day was near
when he'd become a star
and make the grandest entry
on the stage inside the jar

he moved the TV to one side
and microwaved his lunch
washed the dishes in the sink
and finished off the punch

tidied up his living room
vacuumed every floor
dusted off the furniture
and polished every door

soon the big day was at hand
as family gathered 'round
cedric burst upon the stage
and never made a sound

wendy watching everything
spread out upon a cloth
puckered up her faced and cried
"oh mommy, he's a moth!"

cedric felt just horrible
he turned to hide his face
spread his brownish mothy wings
and left in deep disgrace

he flew along and got quite lost–
so stopped to make a choice
and from behind clearly heard
a most attractive voice

cedric turned around to see
a girl moth just like him–
fluttered over next to her
and sat upon a limb

now cedric is a married moth
his life a "cater-thriller"
a gorgeous wife and seven
little baby caterpillars

if someone calls you funny names
and makes you feel quite blue
learn the lesson cedric did–
there's someone just like you!

My Dad

My dad would look so handsome
with a moustache and a beard—
But if you want to know the truth
my dad is sort of weird!

He tinkers with the furnace
in our basement by the hour—
And sings a very silly song
each morning in the shower!

He wired a YOWEE in the wall
to fix my broken light—
And when the YOWEE bit his hand
he yelled in pure delight!

I know my dad had lots of fun
the time my shower leaked—
Because he fixed it many times
and stretched it out a week!

His laugh is very funny
but his jokes are kind of dumb—
And once I heard him holler
when he hammered on his thumb!

My dad is kind of different
but he has the softest touch—
I love him cause he's different—
Yes, I love my dad so much!

Computer Frog

There's a frog on my computer
sticky rubber, soft and green—
There's a frog on my computer
and he's climbing on the screen!

I can see his rubber fingers
as I try to sit and type—
And just because his legs are fake
still doesn't make it right!

There's a frog on my computer—
Not a real one, just the same
There's a frog on my computer
I don't even know his name!

Papalopolis

There was an place in ancient Greece
So poets reminisce
A place so dear, yet far from here
Named Papalopolis
Its houses built on good advice
Its roads with ageless stone
Its halls of granite ever strong
Its walls by sweat and bone
A democratic band, they were
Whose mindful use of power
Taught their young benevolence
When it became *their* hour
A city state that seemed to know
When times were getting tough
And how much extra love to give
When words were not enough
I know these things, for I have seen
Its ancient crumbling halls
And read the letters fairly wrote
Upon its aged walls–

> *O'Papalopolis, we come*
> *In times of great travail–*
> *To place our trust, in you we must*
> *For goodness to prevail*
> *Though ages come and ages go*
> *And stone and bone dissolve–*
> *Held above by godly love*
> *Our culture must evolve*

I wonder if they're watching now
On Olympus' cloudy heights–
And look to see one such as me
Stand reverent in the night
For though I am a modern man
And do not know their names
What they had, those sons and dads–
Lives in *me* just the same

Dynamite-Bill

Dynamite-Bill had a place on a hill
That exploded and blew off his wig
It flew up so high in the cold winter sky
and landed on Fredrick the pig
The pig looked around at the sky and the ground
 to see how he finally got hair
Then opened a shop called "Bottom and Top"
to peddle toupees by the pair

THE PAISLEY PUFFYN POEMS

If you are a puddle duck,
Or quilted "wanna-be".
Look inside this simple guide—
And learn to be like me!

—Paisley Puffyn

Paisley Puffyn in "Judge Puddle Duck"

Wendy had gone off to school
In winter coat and hat—
Mother in her office worked,
Cassandra down for nap

In Wendy's room a silence laid
About the chair and bed
Until a shy and tiny voice
From the silence said—

Order! Order in the court!
Quilties take your chairs!
Let's begin to hear the case
Of Wadsworth Teddy Bear

Justice Paisley Puffyn Puddle
Waddled in the door—
In a powdered wig and robe
That dragged along the floor

Wadsworth Bear, over there
Has come before the court
So we can see (and know if he)
Has been a stingy sort!

Charges brought before us
Say Bear just wouldn't share
And witnessing against him
Is Cuddle Bunny Hare

The jury was assembled
They numbered only nine
And being neat, took a seat
To form a single line

A turtle Felix Hardshell
A panda black and white
Sidney snake, Jake the rake
A dinosaur named Dwight

A pink flamingo Reginald
Gracie kangaroo
Alexander penguin
And Alabaster Shrew

Quilties I shall rule today
With expert legal zeal—
As the court tries to sort
Which charges may be real

As you Quilties surely know
A trial takes more than luck
Therefore I must tell you—
I'm a skillful legal duck!

Do you Hare, right over there
Swear to tell the truth?

Yes I do, I really do—
But why would I tell Ruth?

Ruth? Ruth? I said the truth!
Try a second time—

Oh, the truth? I wouldn't lie—
For it would be a crime!

Just tell the court your story
And try to keep it short
We all know Bear didn't share—
It's here in your report!

Wendy left some cookies
One each for me and Bear
And when I went to eat one
There wasn't any there!

Bear, you must be guilty
The Bunny wouldn't lie
The only thing to tell the court
Is just your reason why

Madame Justice, said the Bear
I didn't take her snac
She took my cookie and I'm here
To fairly get it back!
Hare, you must be guilty
The Bear just wouldn't lie
The only thing to tell the court
Is just your reason why

I didn't take his cookie!
He simply must be witless—
And to prove my story true
I'll call my bestest witness!

A hush fell on the courtroom
A little hare hopped in
She sat her bottom on the chair
Not sure where she'd begin

She was a tiny lop-ear
With floppy ears so funny
All the Quilties knew her as—
Cassandra's little Bunny

Quilties of the jury
This is my sister Bunny
Please beware she's a hare
Whose nose is very runny

Bunny tell the jury—
And Quilties everywhere
About dear Wendy's cookies
That Bear just wouldn't share

Yeth, the lop-eared Bunny said
Tears welled in her eyes
Cookieth yummby on the bed
Gif Bunny big surprith!

That's enough! It's quite enough!
Justice Puffyn said—
It's quite apparent that the Bear
Took them off the bed!

The court has reached decision
I'm giving my report—
Before she could continue
Little Bunny stopped her short

Yeth my cookieth big surprith
Make Bunny vewy hungwy
Cookieth Hungwy Bunny be—
Yummby in my tummby!

Quilties started laughing
Jumped and hugged and kissed
Paisley slammed her gavel down
And shouted *CASE DISMISSED!*

Bear, I'm really sorry
Hare I'm sorry too
Will you please forgive me
The way you always do?

And when the ruckus settled down
And Quilties went to bed
Paisley Puffyn Puddle Duck
To the others said—

It's good that I could listen—
And make some legal quacks
Contemplate the evidence
And verify the facts!

Yes my simple quilted friends
It's wise you turned to me—
And found with luck a justice duck
That rules with dignity!

Paisley Puffyn as Doctor Puffyn Puddle
In "Wendy Gets the Flu"

The morning dawned in Wendy's room
just like any other
But not like every other day
when Wendy called her mother—

Mommy, please come quickly!
I'm feeling very poor
My tummy aches, my face is hot
my throat is very sore!
Hmmm, said Wendy's mother
I'd say you have the flu
You have a fever; one-o-three
just what are we to do?
I'm just not sure how I feel
first I'm hot then cool
Perhaps it's best to get some rest
and not go in to school

So mother brewed some special tea
to take the chill away
Propped some toys upon the bed
to pass the time away
Paisley Puffyn Puddle Duck
was placed upon the bed
Silken scarf around her neck
and bonnet on her head
Cuddle Bunny Hare was there
and Wadsworth Teddy Bear
Each snuggled on the pillow
tangled up in Wendy's hair

Now usually the fun would start
with Wendy acting silly
By throwing Bear into the air
and laughing willy-nilly
But nothing seemed to happen
Wendy didn't even budge
So Bear and Hare together there
gave the girl a nudge

Bear, I'm very worried
Wendy never acts this way
Most all the time, rain or shine
she always wants to play!

Cuddle Bunny looking sad[16A]
soon began to cry
And wouldn't stop no matter what
Wadsworth Bear would try
Then hare began to panic
her sobbing getting worse
And shouted high up to the sky
Oh please, WE NEED A NURSE!

A NURSE, my nervous quilted friends,
would only make a muddle—
But you're in luck to have a duck
like DOCTOR PUFFYN PUDDLE!

As Paisley stood before them
the others couldn't speak—
They'd never seen a doctor duck
with glasses on her beak
She wore a stocking on her head
and laboratory coat
And something like a stethoscope
hung down around her throat

Hare had stopped her crying
and Bear laid on the bed
They couldn't keep from laughing
until the doctor said—

Laugh my friends, just go ahead
laugh until you burst
While I learn the kind of germ
that makes her feel the worst!
For while you're acting silly
and helping not the least
I will still, by force of will
defeat the flu-like beast!

The good physician Puddle Duck
examined Wendy's head
Felt her ears, tweaked her nose
touched her skin and said—

Hmmm…Oh yes, of course, I see
it's just as I surmised
She's got the flu, I'm telling you
it comes as no surprise
In doctor talk (she made a squawk)
we call it "tummyosis"—
And Wendy's case (she made a face)
confirms my diagnosis!

Then Cuddle Bunny Hare replied
Wendy's not in school
And I fear THE END IS NEAR
because her skin is cool!

How true it is, poor little girl
she is ill indeed—
Shivering with fever chills
warmth is what she needs
All right my fellow Quilties,
we've a yeoman's job this day—
Follow me and plainly see
the role you each must play!

Doctor Puffyn Puddle led
the Quilties off the bed
Over to the furnace vent
and to the others said—
Sit here on this heater
warm your bottoms extra hot
I will call you to the bed
and show you to your spot

So each one as their turn came
climbed upon the bed
And snuggled close to Wendy
in the place that Paisley said.

Bear you go down underneath
the covers to her skin
Put your body close to her
and let the heat soak in!
Hare you climb the pillow
to a spot right over there
Place your heated bunny tail
under Wendy's hair

So the Quilties took their turns
throughout the afternoon
And kept the heat upon her feet
to make her better soon
And when her mother tiptoed in
to check her little one—
She found her extra snuggly warm
and eager for some fun

Mommy, I feel better
but I had the strangest dream—
A pretty angel warmed me
with a magic angel beam

Rest my little precious one
rest and close your eyes—
Let the angel keep you safe
until the morning rise

Mother left her little one
asleep and feeling well
Tiptoed from the quiet room
as darkness softy fell

A *hush,* a stillness settled in
and covered all the bed
As Paisley Puffyn Puddle Duck
to the others said—

There my steadfast quilted friends
I've saved the day again—
And with a quirk of doctor work
Wendy's on the mend
So learn a simple lesson
from a doctor duck like me—
It takes a duck with poise and pluck
to earn a doctor's fee!

Paisley Puffyn in "Case of the Purple Yarn"

What is it Hare? A stringy-string? Or something extra-rare?
From a corner by the desk said Wadsworth Teddy Bear
Oh goodness me! Oh gracious be, it gives me quite a scare!
From the bedpost of the bed, squealed Cuddle Bunny Hare
For there before them on the floor a serpent with no head—
A stringy-string of purple yarn wound underneath the bed
Far within the darkest dark, the yarn soon disappeared
And left them shivering with fright and cowering in fear

What is the ruckus there below? A voice called from the bed
Paisley Puffyn Puddle Duck, a bonnet on her head
What have you there, Mr. Bear? A purple stringy-string?
Perhaps a path to pirate gold…we should trail that thing!
What you need, my quilted friends, is one with grand finesse
You're in luck; Inspector Duck will see you through this mess!

Paisley Puffyn squiggled down and took the yarn in hand
Raised her magnifying glass to survey every strand
Oh yes, of course! I see! Ah-ha! It all seems very clear
It seems the stringy-string's a path to what we so revere!
You'll notice that my finest stitch is of a purple thread
And matches all that stringy-string that leads beneath the bed

So Paisley…No, Inspector Duck, led Quilties with a quack
To find the place where pirate gold lay buried on the track
So silently and carefully they crawled beneath the bed
Inspector Paisley Puffyn Duck, a flashlight on her head

Please, don't leave me last in line…I've had a little scare
Said Cuddle Bunny as she budged right in front of Bear
No you don't! No you won't, take my place in line!
Said Wadsworth Bear, pushing Hare hard on her behind.
Quilties! Quilties! That's enough! Must you twice be told?
You're on a quest with me (the best) to search for pirate gold!
Look there, far ahead of us, a pair of Wendy's socks
and stringy-string is leading us into that cardboard box!

Paisley…uh, Inspector Duck, it goes into a hole
Wadsworth said filled with dread, *What if there's a troll?*

A troll? A troll? In that hole? That would be the worst!
Just in case that is the case, Bear you go in first!

What? Me the first? That is the worst! I cannot go in there!
If anyone should have the fun, I think it should be Hare!

Oh no, not me, you plainly see that I am short on luck
If anyone should have the fun, it's good Inspector Duck!

All right, we'll go together. We'll follow stringy-string—
Through the hole, face the troll and treasure out we'll bring

It was so true; the purple yarn did wind around the socks
And led the brave exploring crew inside the cardboard box
Inspector Duck and quilted friends tumbled through the hole
And once within side by side they stood to face the troll

But none could move a muscle, stood frozen just like ice
For nestled snug before them was a nest of baby mice
The purple stringy-stringy yarn was made into their bed
One yawned and squeaked a squeaky-squeak and raised his little head

Inspector Duck had gone away; but Paisley Puffyn stayed
And when the little mice awoke, Quilties played and played

As all good days, it had to end; friends said fond goodbyes
But it was nice for little mice to have a grand surprise
And every after from that time (as far as she could see)
Paisley Puffyn Puddle Duck and mice as friends would be.

Paisley Puffyn in "Rootin' Tootin' Cowgirl"

It always seemed to happen,
With Wendy gone away
Sometimes late in morning
Or middle of the day

With mother in her office
Cassandra fast asleep
Quiet in the bedroom
Quilties start to speak

Listen to me pardners—
Paisley Puffyn said
Bandana tied around her neck
Big hat on her head

We need to be a ridin'—
Though it's wet 'n very foggy
To the range on the plain
To rope a little doggy

Who are you supposed to be?
Asked Cuddle Bunny Hare[16J]
If you ask, SHE'LL TELL US!
Warned Wadsworth Teddy Bear

I am, my simple quilted friend)
Montana Puffyn Puddle—
And ride (of course) upon a horse
Named Aloysius Tuttle

Paisley went behind the bed
And dragged him out by force—
The biggest, reddest, wildest
Buckin' bronco hobbyhorse!

Ah'm goin' ropin' doggies
And leavin' right away—
But first I need some sidekicks
For the trip to Santa Fe!

Bear and Hare were happy—
We'll stay close by your side!
I mean we'll be your partners
And join you on the ride!

Steady Aloysius—
Montana Puffyn said
And set her frame on the mane
Behind the horse's head

Montana held the bridle
Wadsworth sat up tall
Cuddle Bunny pushy-pushed
Aloysius down the hall

Whoa! Montana shouted—
Far out on the range
We are very far home
This range is mighty strange!

Carefully and quietly
They crept into a room
Leaving Aloysius tied
Outside to a broom

Once inside Wadsworth cried
Look out! A giant horse!
Quilties dove beneath the bed—
Why? To hide, of course!

The giant horse dipped his head
To where the Quilties hid
With his nose, sniffed each one
Until Montana said—
Mr. Horse, we (of course)
Are cowboys from afar
Could you please direct us
And tell us where we are?

The giant horse seemed angry
His nose and whiskers dark
He looked right at the Quilties—
And gave a muffled BARK!

What did the giant horsey say?
Cuddle Bunny asked
BARK is what I think he said—
What kind of horse says that?

Silly Puffyn! He's a dog!
His name is Boxer King
His job is to protect me—
From almost anything

Who was that? Wadsworth asked
Looking toward the bed
And peeking from the covers
Was a toddler's little head

I'm Cassandra, you must be—
The little toddler said
Quilted friends from Wendy's room
That wandered from her bed?

Why yes we are, Paisley paused
Somewhat taken back
We didn't know that little girls
Could talk in "quilted quacks"

Why yes, all little boys and girls
All little girls like me—
Can talk to you in "quilted quacks"
Until we're nearly three

How do you do? I'm only two—
And hear you very clear
So I can talk in "quilted quacks"
At least another year!

You see we all get lonely
When we are very small
So God just lets us talk to you
And Quilties one and all

Paisley looked around the room
From furniture to chai.
And with surprise saw the eyes
Of other Quilties there!

There was Alice Elephant
Tuxedo Panda Bear
Wiley Frog and Wendell Dog
And Fuzzy Bunny Hare

Well Cassandra, little one—
I reckon' we'll be goin'
There's bulls to ride, broncs to bust—
And doggies that need ropin'

Aloysius hobbyhorse
Stood beside the wall
Quilties climbed upon his back
And rode on down the hall

Quilties got down off his back
And found some purple thread
Then Montana tied his reins
To the bedpost of the bed

Wendy would be home from school
So Quilties climbed aloft
And Paisley Puffyn Puddle Duck
To the others scoffed—

There my simple quilted friends
I've seen you through a muddle
And taught you many cowboy things
On Aloysius Tuttle

It's just your luck you have a duck
Who knows the cowboy way
And tamed the giant horsey
On the road to Santa Fe!

PAISLEY PUFFYN COMES TO TEA

"And such *delicious* sipping tea," Paisley Puffin said–
Silken scarf around her neck and bonnet on her head.

"It's just about the *finest* tea," Agreed Wadsworth the Bear.
"And not a teeny bit too strong," Said Cuddle Bunny Hare.

"Why, thank you very, very much," Said Wendy with a smile.
"I'm glad to have you come to tea and stay and talk awhile."

Wendy hosted many teas for all her dearest friends–
And ever to her grand delight, they always would attend.

For Paisley Puffin, Wadsworth Bear and Cuddle Bunny Hare–
Were animals just stuffed with stuff and propped up in a chair.

Wendy took them from the bed and set them down for tea.
Dressed them in their finest clothes for everyone to see.

"Won't you have a cookie, Bear?" Asked with glad appeal–
Mother overhearing said, "You know, they're just not real."

Wendy put them on the bed and sadly left for town.
And all the rest of party time, her friends made not a sound.

A quiet covered all the room; the chairs, the desk, the bed.
A silence round the table laid, until a shy voice said–

"And such *delicious* sipping tea," Did Paisley Puffin say.
"Would you like a cookie, Bear, with Wendy gone away?"

"Oh thank you, very, very much," Replied Wadsworth the Bear.
"I'm sure this is the *grandest* tea," Squealed Cuddle Bunny Hare.

Fond "good-byes" went all around, hugs from friend to friend–
And left each other once again with tea time at an end.

So Paisley Puffin left her chair and climbed back on the bed–
A silken scarf around her neck and bonnet on her head.

PAISLEY PUFFYN
GOES TO CAMP

Wendy mailed a letter with a thirty-four cent stamp,
scribbled on the envelope "Sleepy Apple Camp."
Dropped it in the mailbox on the corner of the street,
packed her purple camping bag, snuggled down to sleep.

Stuffed inside were shoes and socks, flannel underwear–
Paisley Puffin Puddle Duck, Cuddle Bunny Hare.
Shirts and shorts and comic books, bows for pretty hair–
dental floss and candy mints, Wadsworth Teddy Bear.
Paisley Puffin wore her dress - of Piccadilly red,
silken scarf around her neck and bonnet on her head.

"Sleepy Apple Bus" careened along the road to camp,
turned the corner at the light, jostled down the ramp,
stopped to let the kids off, excitement calming down,
quiet settled on the group and Paisley looked around.

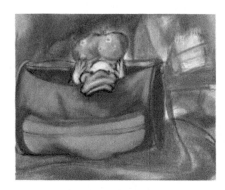

Her purple bag opened up, a quilted head stuck out.
Paisley Puffin looked in shock at what was all about–
Her camping bag was on a cot with other cots around,
clustered in a canvas tent plopped upon the ground.
"Should a lady have to stay in such a dingy place?
Hardly any room for clothes in such a tiny space!"

"Geronimo!" Wadsworth called, leaping from the pack,
tumbled down the nylon slope square on Paisley's back.
Cuddle Bunny Hare was next, pouncing on the bed,
tried to do a somersault and landed on his head–
"Gracious me," Paisley grumped, angered by the fray,
stuck her nose up in the air and waddled far away.

Every pack on every cot began to split to shreds,
animals of every kind were bouncing on the beds–
Quilted dogs and elephants, purple kangaroos,
spotted bears and golden mares, iridescent shrews.

"Look at them," Paisley grumped, with a haughty quack,
using stubby puffin wings to climb inside the pack.
Down she sat in deep disgust, chaos reined below,
bouncing ever carelessly, jumping high and low.

Suddenly, laughing heard - kids were coming back!
"Quickly! Quickly!" came the cry, "Back into your packs!"
Some toys made it, others not, most had tried their best–
Wendy and the other kids found their tent a mess!

Peanuts here, Nachos there, licorice everywhere,
Wendy searching in the tent, spotted Wadsworth Bear.
There upon a rumpled cot, ribbons on his head,
Tiny Wadsworth Teddy Bear square upon the bed.
Purple socks over ears, lipstick on his nose,
tennis shoes hiding paws, toothpaste on his clothes.

Cuddle Bunny Hare was found lying on the floor,
firmly stuck with sticky tape to cardboard by the door.

"They really didn't listen," Paisley smugly thought,
acting so uncivilized, begging to get caught!"

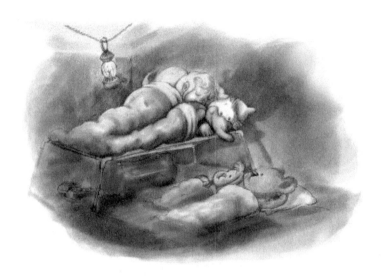

Later in the sleeping bag, snugly on the bed,
Paisley Puffin, ever smug, to the others said–
"Boys, I'm disappointed. You should've stuck with me.
Kept a proper attitude and civilized you'd be.
Remember I'm a puddle duck of high society–
and royal quilted member of the aristocracy!"

PAISLEY PUFFYN

DRESS UP DAY

"HIP HOORAY, TIME FOR FUN!" echoed everywhere
seated high upon the bed with Cuddle Bunny Hare,
was Paisley Puffyn Puddle Duck, suave and debonair,
sitting on the dresser, tiny Wadsworth Teddy Bear.

Wendy went away to school, dolls were having fun,
Hide-and-Seek, Simon Says, 'Round the Pillow Run.
"Fellow Quilties," Paisley said, tugging at her sleeve,
"The only game I will play is *Dress up Make-Believe*."

Her comment signaled everyone to tumble to the floor,
race across the shaggy rug and through the closet door.
Rummage boxes packed inside, pull out all the stuff ;
clothes and hats, baby toys, Wendy's fluffy muff.

Wadsworth Bear chose to wear overalls and tails,
dress-up shoes on his feet, polish on his nails.
"How DO you do?" Wadsworth asked, with a haughty flare.
"Will you come have some tea?" Nose up in the air.

Cuddle Bunny Hare had picked a purple curly wig,
Stretchy funny leotards, dancing shoes TOO BIG.
"A ballet bunny from afar!" Tipping on her toes.
"La-La-La, I am a star," tripping on her clothes.
Quilties jumping up and down, falling on the ground,
turning topsy somersaults, spinning clear around.

"Now I'll show you how to dress," Paisley Puffyn said.
Took the scarf from her neck and bonnet off her head.

"As for me, you mustn't look," Paisley softly said.
She made the others hide their eyes and wait behind the bed.
"All right, it's time," Paisley chimed, "You may take a look."
Wadsworth Bear and ballet Hare laughed until they shook.
For there upon the shaggy rug, and goodness, what a sight!
Paisley Puffyn Puddle Duck was dressed in orange tights.
Yellow mask around her eyes, sweatshirt on her back,
purple "P" upon her chest, cape of midnight black.

"Who are you?" Wadsworth asked, with a silly grin.

"Are you slow? Don't you know? I am SUPER PUFFYN!"

She started fast, well fast for her, waddling on the floor,
lost her balance landing on a skateboard by the door.
"HELP!" she cried, terrified, racing down the hall,
rolling fast, when at last, she crashed into the wall.
"Oh, my head," she complained, and waddled back inside.
Then with a smile on her face..."Goodness, what a ride!"

Late at night with Wendy snuggled warmly in her bed,
Paisley Puffyn Puddle Duck to the others said,
"I really am a SUPER PUFFYN, I must surely be
the best dressed puffyn puddle duck in high society.
So take a fashion lesson from a duck with dignity.
Super hero clothes are "in" for such a star as me!"

RAYMOND COPP

PAISLEY PUFFYN
GOES TO SCHOOL

"Today's the day!" Paisley quacked,
Poised upon the bed.
Silken scarf around her neck
And bonnet on her head.

Paisley Puffyn Puddle Duck
Was really feeling cool–
Knowing it was "Show and Tell"
Today at Wendy's school.

The bag was stuffed with school supplies
And other odds and ends.
Like books and lunch and homework jobs,
And very special friends.

For Paisley Puffyn Puddle Duck
And Cuddle Bunny Hare.
Were quickly, snugly stuffed inside
Along with Wadsworth Bear.

Inside the bag, it sure was dark,
As dark as darkest night–
Tempers flared, the school bus bumped,
And friends began to fight!

"My ears are bent!" Cried the hare,
"You're feet are in my face!
My nose is sore, my tail is mushed
MOVE OVER, GIVE ME SPACE!"

The classroom was a clamor,
A real cacophony–
That's a word for lots of noise,
And rhymes with symphony.

Wendy's turn was near the end,
In fact, she was the last.
And as she pulled the bag apart,
The children gave a gasp!

For Cuddle Bunny Hare was tied
To Wadsworth by his nose.
Dental floss around his legs
And pudding on his clothes!

There must have been an awful fight,
The bag was such a mess.
And who was left for "Show and Tell?"
 I'll give you just *one* guess–

The last to make her entrance
Into school society.
Was Paisley Puffyn Puddle Duck,
As grand as she could be.

She moved along to center stage
With such a graceful ease.
Turned and strutted back again
As regal as you please.

The children loved her eveningwear
Of Piccadilly red.
Silken scarf around her neck
And bonnet on her head.

And when they were at home again,
Snug upon the bed.
Paisley Puffyn looked around,
And to the others said–

"Such a lovely day it was,
The audience was grand.
So thoughtful too, as I was through,
To give me such a hand."

"Next time I'll ask our Wendy dear,
To drive *me* in the car–
For that would be the *proper* way
To treat a movie star!"

A Puddle Duck Guide to Childcare

Paisley Puffyn gives wise advice to stuffed animals on how to care for children

All wonders of the universe
All stars in heaven too—
Softly say, they're made that way
Especially for you

For each of you along the way
Will have a special friend
One that you can understand—
Whose secrets you will tend

So if you are a quilted friend
Or Puffyn puddle duck—
It's best that you remember
Life takes *more* than luck

Manners

This book is full of stories
By expert puddle ducks
Like Paisley Puffyn's essay
Of Tea Time run amok—

The first thing to remember
Before you get too wild—
Is that your obligation
Is to your special child

Love is your assignment
The reason you were sewn
To love and hold and cuddle—
Until your child is grown

You may encounter teatime
With plastic cups and spoons
And sit around a table
Throughout the afternoon

Your place is not to criticize
Nor should you make correction

Wait your turn, the child will learn—
From your best direction!

I remember one fine day
With Wendy gone away—
Wadsworth Bear and Cuddle Hare
Came for lunch and play

Their manners were atrocious
If fact, they spelled disaster
And but for me, a lovely tea
Would have ended faster!

So the rule is keep your cool
Patience here is good
A child will take sound advice
As they rightly should!

Fashion

A "Quiltie" is a special friend
Made with love and thread
Propped up on a pillow
At the far end of the bed

As Paisley Puffyn tells us
With some degree of luck
When picking stylish clothing
Fashion makes the duck—

You could be a movie star
Or sailor from Japan
A salesman from Milwaukee
Or the princess of Siam!
You see, in every puddle duck
A thousand actors live
Change a hat and just like that
A grand performance give!

Health Care

Since your child is helpless
Yours to guide with skill
She may need assistance
Beating fever's chill

Expert on the subject
Here to clear the muddle
Is a duck that's seldom stuck
Good Doctor Puffyn Puddle—

Students take advice from me—
(And sit up in your seats)
For the flu and fever too
It's best to give some heat

Starve a fever, feed a cold
Is what I always say
Feed your child chicken soup
And you could save the day!

Let's review all we've learned
From this our teaching spree
Feed them soup, be concerned
And charge a handsome fee!

Security

You may encounter mystery
Confusing children's minds
It falls to you to follow through
And finally solve the crime

It may not be too easy
And may take special luck
Expert commentary comes
From good Inspector Duck—

Ahem... my young detectives
I am Inspector Duck
And spend my time fighting crime
With special poise and pluck.

I cannot stress it hard enough
That crime just doesn't pay
For bad guys making mischief
In the middle of the day

A super sleuth will learn the truth
If she is in her prime
And send the poor offenders
Off to jail to do their time!

Leadership

Children's rooms often have
Fifty toys or more
From red raccoons to blue baboons
To soldiers by the score

From chaos, order seldom comes
In bedrooms small or large
Until a Puffyn puddle duck
Elects to be in charge

Often leaders come along
From Quilties made to cuddle
A duck who stands above the rest
Is Justice Puffyn Puddle—

Fairness! Fairness! That's the word
When sitting as a judge
Never ever change your mind
Don't even make a budge

You will know what is the truth
Before the trial begins
Don't let softy quiltie types
Change your mind again!

Fairness! Fairness! Every time
That's the word to use
And never let the evidence
Effect the way you choose!!

Facing Fear

The last one is important,
For Quilties one and all
Danger, fear and scary threats
Lay hidden in the hall

It's up to you to find them
Outside the bedroom door
Confront them bravely face-to-face
And knock them to the floor

One among your number
A puddle in a muddle
Is western duck and cowboy star
Montana Puffyn Puddle—

Howdy little puddlers
Ah just got back from ridin'
On the range actin' strange
A thinkin' 'n decidin'

About a doggy ah should rope
And broncos needin' bustin'
Of skunks 'n low down filthy rats—
That ah cannot be trustin'

So round up little doggies
Herd them down the floor
Lasso all yer worries—
And drive them out the door

Someday when you're older
Your stitching all worn out
You'll reminisce about your life
And what it's been about

The bedroom then deserted
It's all you've ever known
A quiet haunts it all the time—
Your child is fully-grown

And then one day it happens
The door swings open wide
Your special friend before you—
A small child at *her* side

The little one adores you
Holds you though you're old
And even after all these years—
It's worth much more than gold

THE END

THE FILBY BILBY POEMS

This will make your poor heart sink—
Some kinds of bilbies are extinct
and several others on the brink
of disappearing in a wink

Filby Bilby and the Brothers Foo

I came from London to Timboon
looking for some breathing room
and thought that I would never see
a platypus or wallaby

But way back then I didn't know
about the famous flying show
that every night since days of old
near the Southern Cross unfolds

A daring tale of Brothers Foo
and Filby Bilby brave and true—
And how he soared up in the sky
And freed a land from dragonflies

Austrailian children will recall
That bilbies are marsupials—-
Which simply means they have a pouch
a kind of undercover couch

A place to feed their babies lunch
and keep them snug in one tight bunch
So kids down under you may snooze
while other children hear the news
about your bilbies and their kind
and then our story can unwind

For other children round the earth
Far away from York or Perth
like foggy London or Nepal—
Who don't know very much at all
about the bilbies and their land—
This may help them understand

Bilbies are just bunny-size
with longish ears and darkish eyes
and a pink and pointy nose
with blue-gray fur instead of clothes

Their furry tails of black and white
Make them such a funny sight—
They only show themselves at night
for sunshine gives them awful fright

Their eyes are poor; they don't see well
but how their little noses smell
and love the sport of digging down
underneath the night time ground—
And any food will make them sing
for bilbies eat most anything

Like tasty grubs or buzzing flies
or hopping toads with bulging eyes
or crickets chirping in the night
or any insect in their sight

But this will make your poor hearts
sink—
Some kinds of bilbies are extinct
and several others on the brink
of disappearing in a wink—

Australian children come back in
It's time our story did begin

One fine day, I walked along
and whistled out a happy song—
When all at once an aeroplane
one so small, I can't explain
from where it came or how it flew—
But oh the things that plane could do
like loop and roll and twist and spin
and sail along upon the wind—

And when it swooped down for a pass
where I could hear the pilot laugh
and clearly see his happy face—
I knew that bilbies loved to race

His aeroplane was bluish-green
with two fat wings and in between
some little poles to hold them tight
like wooden sticks tied on a kite

There was a cockpit to sit in
whose top was open to the wind—
A big propeller on the nose
just like a fan to make it go

And when that plane began to sail
I saw some writing on the tail—
Ugly bugs make you nervous?
Call Filby Bilby Flying Service

He flashed a grin, held out a paw
and that's the first time that I saw—
He wore old goggles and a hat
with longish ears stuck out like that

And then I knew— it struck me plain
this daring bilby and his plane
were flying stars (that's for sure)—
And should take a worldwide tour

One time in China, in Hanshu
Filby met the "Brothers Foo"
who were the terror of the skies
because the Foos were dragonflies

These insects of enormous size
with big and scary purple eyes—
And bodies that were green and black
with horrid wings stuck on their back

The Brother Foos had ruled the land
with members of their dragon clan
and terrorized all kinds of birds
and often shouted ugly words—
And dove down fast to scoop up cats
and tiny squirrels and Beijing rats—

So even children were afraid
when Brothers Foo went on a raid

"Be careful bilby!" Someone said—
But Filby laughed and shook his head
his engine roaring, splitting smoke
he shouted loud a daring joke—

Clear the way, you Brothers Foo—
Flyin' Filby's comin' through!

It was a challenge of the air
but Foos were bad and didn't care—
With ugly friends they came at night
and Filby Bilby had to fight

He calmly flew his sturdy craft
and looped and rolled and gave a laugh
and when the Foos made one attack
he rolled that plane upon its back—

As each Foo passed but couldn't stop
he chewed their wings off with his prop!

The crowd below made "aahs" and
"oohs"
as Filby beat the Brothers Foo!

Foos crashed in fields and in a creek
into the mud and in the street
into the river and a lake
And after that all he'd take—

As pay for freeing them from Foos
was ice cream bars and chocolate ooze!

Then Filby flew back home to stay
Just west of Perth near Wally's Bay—
And if you ask of Brothers Foo
he'll tell his story just for you—

And there I was up in the sky
so all-alone and very high—
Danger round me left and right
My only choice was stand and fight

zSo many fiercesome Brothers Foo
I did not know quite what to do—
Then I remembered and took out
the bubblegum stored in my pouch

I chewed the gum into a ball
and the one thing I recall
was a bubble meters wide
with a Foo trapped tight inside

And when I saw the trick work once
I used it on the whole bad bunch!

Now it's too bad you have nowhere
To store your gum or teddy bear

But China's glad that bilbies do—
For that's the way I beat the Foos!"

Filby Bilby and the Cuckoo Bees

I came from Texas to Maree
lookin' for a wallaby—
Instead I found a platypus
koala bear and octopus

And animals of every size
with scaly skin or scary eyes
making growls or groans or cries
and soon I came to realize—
Chasing them was so unwise

One dark night I got a scare
from a buzzing in the air—
And found it hardest to explain
those bilbies flying aeroplanes!

Most bilbies love to tunnel down
underneath the daytime ground—
But in the night Australian sky
how those bilbies love to fly

They dive and turn and whirl and loop
and spin and twist and curve and swoop
and soar and glide as night begins
to ride the current of the winds

Australians think the bilby shy
but seldom look up to the sky
and see the tiny airplanes there
buzzing in the nighttime air

I often watched them flying there
soaring high without a care—
So it will come as no surprise
their flying seemed to hypnotize
the crowd of watchers on the ground
staring up without a sound
A special bilby caught my eye
turning, swirling in the sky—

One so cool and debonair
flying with a cowboy's flair

Filby Bilby was his name
and he flew a fancy plane—
Flying goggles on his eyes
a shabby jacket just his size

He had a long and pinkish snout
and wore a hat with ears stuck out
and hidden deep within his pouch
some secret stuff that poked about

Filby's plane was bluish-green
with two big wings and in-between
some struts and wires to hold them tight
and little lights to see at night
to help him keep the bugs in sight—
Because the one thing he did right
was feed his healthy appetite!

And when he landed, dare I say
I offered him a job with pay—
And we became the best of friends
and toured the world from end to end

We made a stop in Santa Fe
back in the good old USA—
Where Filby gave an awesome show
to some cowboys down below—
Standing watching in their chaps
cowboy boots and Stetson hats—
A daring bilby looping round
over, under, upside down

As Filby made his final loop
a swarm of bees came down to swoop
with a rope tied in a loop
a little bird right off his stoop
and dropped him in a soupy goop
They yipped and hollered
yelled and cussed
screamed and shouted
fussed and mussed—
As wild as any bugs could be
were the nasty Cuckoo Bees

I helped the bird wipe off the goop
untied the rope, undid the loop
and asked why bees would rudely swoop
a little bird right off his stoop
and drop him in such nasty goop

But when he looked me in the eye
that little bird began to cry—
Tears ran down along his beak
to fall in puddles at his feet

He told a tale of Cuckoo Bees
that laid in wait in scrubby trees
to ambush all who happened by—
Diving on them from the sky

Cuckoo Bees were lazy lugs
that terrorized most other bugs
and little birds and butterflies
and tiny mice with frightened eyes—
Who would swoop or chase or sting
a long-horn steer or anything

The leader's name was "Bandit Buzz"
a badder bee there never was—
As bad as any bee could be
from Santa Fe to old Fort Lee

With faded black and yellow bands
fuzzy legs and sticky hands—
The baddest bad and meanest mean
of any bee you've ever seen

Cuckoos threatened awful stings
and hated almost everything—
They flew in swarms to show their might
while other bugs would hide in fright

I had hung on every word
of the frightened little bird—
Who told about the Cuckoo Bees
hiding in the scrubby trees

As Filby Bilby stood nearby
a single tear fell from his eye—
And hung suspended on his nose
before it dripped down on his toes

I don't suppose you've ever had
the chance to see a bilby mad—
The fur stands up behind their head
and then their face gets very red
and knowing Filby, I could see—
It was best to leave him be

With flyin' goggles on his eyes
and shabby jacket just his size—
He slapped his plane upon the side
and hollered loud "Come on, let's ride!"

The engine roared, his airplane shook
and Filby with an angry look
took off to find the scrubby trees
and gather up the Cuckoo Bees

They heard him coming far away
and swarmed together on that day
to bring about the final end—
Of my brave Australian friend

A crowd had gathered for the show
to watch the circus from below—
"Fly amigos!" Bandit cried
as angry bees took to the sky

Cuckoos buzzed and twirled and spun
and dove on Filby from the sun—
But he scared that group of bees
and chased 'em back into the trees

To Filby this was loads of fun
to scare the bees and make them run—
For if the bees had known his kind
or if they could have read his mind—
They would've sprinted for the trees
for bilbies love the taste of bees!

Now bilbies have a special pouch
which often times can help them out—
It's where they store so many things
like coils of rope and bits of string

So Filby dug down in his pouch
and found some rope to swing about—
And Cuckoos didn't know it yet
that bilbies are such experts at—
Roping bees with lariats!

"YAHOO!" Filby shouted loud
drawing laughter from the crowd
then sitting high up on the seat
flew the plane with just his feet

Filby let his lasso sail
and snagged a Cuckoo by the tail—
Who squirmed and wiggled, yelled and cried
but not before he'd been hogtied!

"HELP!" the Cuckoo cried in fear
as the earth raced ever near—
He would have died, smashed with ease
if he hadn't hit those trees

One by one the Cuckoos Bees
tumbled helpless to the trees—
And hung there swinging from each limb
snugly tied and looking grim

The last to fall was Bandit Buzz
who crashed into the plane because
he knew that bilbies couldn't fly
outside their airplanes in the sky

That horrid crash was very loud
and drew a *gasp* from all the crowd—
The plane was crippled, wouldn't glide
and little Filby would have died—
But Bandit made one more attack
and Filby jumped onto his back!

The watching crowd made "oohs" and "eees"
as Filby rode that Cuckoo Bee
across the sky and toward the trees
and all the cowboys yelled with glee—
"Ride 'em Filby! Ride that bee!
Ride 'em cowboy, Yes Siree!"

What did he do to Bandit Buzz?
Well, tied him to a tree because—
With some pliers from his pouch
he pulled each Cuckoo's stinger out!

He made them promise to be good
And each one sobbed and said he would
So Filby took them from each tree
untied the ropes and set them free—

And even nasty Bandit Buzz
promised to be good because
without a stinger he was small—
And not a big bug after all

So now the land near Santa Fe
is not as wild in one small way—
Cuckoo Bees were changed a lot
and opened up an ice cream shop

And though the Bees no longer prey
on helpless birds along the way
I guess you still could rightly say
the Cuckoo Bees will make you pay

For people come to town each night—
For "Cuckoo's Chocolate Crunch Delight!"
And that's how Filby saved the day
back in the good old USA—

Filby Bilby and the Tambourine Toad

Out in the middle of the African plain
where the sun shines bright and it don't ever rain—
Near the pride of the lion and the elephant herd
where a man can scream and not be heard—
Where a whole world hides without being seen
in a land near-forgotten called the Tambourine

Long after dark with the moon overhead
and the biggest of creatures already in bed—
The plain comes alive with lovers of night
like snakes and spiders and bats in flight—
But even spiders make a path around
a small night creature moving over the ground

One who's short and squat and fat
but doesn't have fangs or things like that
But coughs and spits and drools and slurps
and gulps his food and rudely burps
And slobbers and gobbles his "moth ala-mode"—
And that's all there is to the Tambourine Toad

The Toad eats flies and bugs for food—
And one thing's certain—

He's awfully CRUDE!

The Tambourine Toad is a lonesome sort
his orangish hide has bumps and warts—
With two goggle eyes stuck onto his head
and a long slinky tongue that's painted red

And here's a sample of something he did—
One night a shrew named Willis Kidd
had saved a worm for a midnight treat
when over hopped Toad on his big flat feet—
And grabbed the worm, then gulped it down
with a kind of glurpy-slurpy sound

Far out on the plain in the African heat
where a nighttime creature has to work to eat—
There's a code unspoken with lovers of the night
"Every creature on the plain must be POLITE!"

RUDE is the word for Tambourine Toad
but that's not the worst of the episode—
He had more habits that weren't polite
and it had to do with his appetite

When he ate fat bugs in the shadowy light—
He'd gobbled up slivers of the dark of night!
When he closed his mouth on a bug or a flea
the night got shorter by a minute or three
And the more he ate, the bigger he was—
And he just got bigger and bigger because
the night added flavor to a bug or a worm
but other little creatures never got a turn—
And nights got shorter as the dark slipped away
till the African night was just another day!

Then nighttime lovers couldn't search for food
with the dark eaten up by a toad being rude
So they held a meeting later on by the road
and elected Snake to speak to the toad
and tell him please "Just do what's right"
and give back pieces he'd eaten of the night

"Oh, Good Mr. Toad," called Satchmo Snake—
"It ain't too polite for you to take—
Pieces of night when you eat your food
And only proves your really RUDE!"

"Go home silly snake, and leave me alone
I'll give back nothing I've claimed my own—
The bugs and flies and the slivers of night
all belong to me and you know that's right!"

So a message went out to Wally's Glade
a good day's walk out of Adelaide—
Where a possum snoozed in a drizzly rain
and a bilby worked on his aeroplane

A letter in the post came Monday noon
with a special request—
"OPEN REALLY SOON!"

The note inside was written in fear
the stationery stained by an animal's tear

"Please Mr. Bilby," the frantic letter read—
"Hurry down to Africa before we're dead!
Please, Mr. Bilby, please come quick—
The Tambourine Toad is making us sick!

He's eaten up the night so we can't find food
And making it worse—
He's awfully RUDE!"

He started up the plane and raced for the scene
to the hottest part of Africa, the Tambourine

Filby wore goggles and his old leather hat
a shabby silk scarf and jacket on his back—
Some secret stuff (packed in his pouch)
and blue pantaloons with his feet sticking out

Okee-Pokey Possum packed tools and things
and hung by his tail from the bottom of the wing

They left Adelaide at a quarter to two
and made a quick pit stop in Katmandu—
Across tall mountains in the Kenyan rain
to make a bumpy landing on the African plain

And though the clock read "half past night"
the sun was high with no night in sight—
Daytime creatures were too tired to eat
and the nighttime crew couldn't take the heat—

It looked like the end of the African plain
'less a bilby and possum in an aeroplane
Made Tambourine Toad be polite once more
and give back night he had taken before

With Filby at the stick for an aerial view
finding that Toad wasn't hard to do—
He'd become so big he could not hide
beneath the ground so he sat outside
with sun beating down on his orangish hide
and he got so hot he nearly fried!
The aeroplane flew like an old "tin-lizzy"
and tropical heat made their hair all frizzy—

But Filby's flying kept everyone busy
as the heat of day made the big Toad dizzy
His thoughts were muddled and his mind in a cloud
he began to dream and mumble out loud—

"Toad don care 'bout night goed way
Toad jes play his trombone all day—
And jes don care if de bug dont stay
No one esk Toad if he wan to play
so Toad ate de night right out of de day"

Then Filby held a meeting of the nighttime crew
and told each creature what he had to do

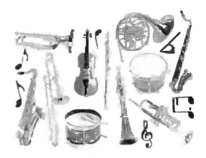

And one by one they asked the Toad
if he'd join a band down by the road—
And Tambourine Toad, dizzy as he was
accepted the chance to play because
he wanted the creatures to treat him nice
so he said "of course" to the snakes and mice

In a dried-up pond as an auditorium
the orchestra stood round the big bass drum—
They waited outside with their saxophones
two base clarinets and a sousaphone—
and danced to a tune on the xylophone
when out hopped Toad with a slide trombone!

Filby stood tall near the dried-up pond
searched his pouch for a bandleader wand—
Tapped it twice and counted to three
and led that band in a grand melody

Satchmo Snake played a smooth coronet
with Willis Kidd on the bass clarinet—
Widow Spider tapped a big bass drum
and kept the rhythm like a pendulum

They played a waltz and some rock-n-roll
a gospel tune and some French Creole—
An Aussie classic 'bout a billabong
and ended up things with a cowboy song

And all were sure of just one thing—
That "Trombone Toad" could really swing!
And every time his note was right—
He blurted-out a little piece of night!

He played it high and played it low
with a tempo fast and a tempo slow—
And everyone yelled "Go Toad Go!"
But the more he played the smaller he growed!

For every waltz or cha-cha-cha
the night got darker with a WAA-WAA-WAA!

And when they paused to watch night fall
the sun disappeared and Toad was small!

And to this day it's not the same
out on the hottest of the African plain—
Where a whole world loves the melodious scene
in a land of music called the Tambourine

Imagine yourself on the darkest night
with only a faint silhouette in sight—
When out of the quiet comes TAP-TAP-TAP
and the voice of a spider "gettin' down" with rap—
Then a horn joins in and then a saxophone
then the OMPHA-PA-PA of a sousaphone—
Then a long fast solo on a xylophone
and "bring it on home" with a slide trombone!

The Tambourine Toad really loves to play
and he'll jam all night and jam all day—
And whenever he hits a note just right
a little more dark creeps into the night

And back "down under" near Wally's Glade—
A good day's walk out of Adelaide

A bilby and possum took a nap in the shade
and thought about the friends they made

And when they drifted off to sleep
with promises they'd yet to keep—
They heard the music of the night
and knew it all had come out right

Filby Bilby on Tour

I came from London just to see
a real live baby wallaby
or kangaroo or some such thing
but never thought I'd ever bring—
A famous bilby back to town
and show him off to all around

Most Australians know by sight
this little creature of the night
That eats fat bugs and crawly things
and creepy insects having wings—
Whose favorite sport is digging down
far beneath the night time ground

People think they're really shy
though seldom look up to the sky—
So few Australians can explain
why bilbies fly their aeroplanes

One fine day, just outside Perth
There soared up high above the earth
an aeroplane with wobbly wings
that looped and rolled and other things

And swooped down low to make a pass
where I could hear the pilot laugh
and plainly see a tattered sign
snugly tied with cotton twine

With writing I could plainly see—
WILL CHASE BUGS FOR A FEE

The engine roared, he swooped again
and people gathered near the glen
to see the fancy flying show
with Filby Bilby diving low

His little plane climbed high again
its cockpit open to the wind
with Filby waving to the crowd
before his plane "popped" through a cloud

You should've seen his furry face
and heard the tired old engine race
and saw him dive and loop and play
and fly that plane in such a way—
That everyone from miles around
stood breathless watching from the ground

I watched him there for quite a while
and when he landed saw him smile—
And then I knew (it was so plain)
this bilby and his aeroplane—
Were going to be big stars for sure
And took them on a worldwide tour

I knew "bug chasing" was his best
when Filby flew in Budapest
and thrilled the crowds in old Cairo
and Istanbul and Hokkaido

He flew that shabby aeroplane
(with a sign that had his name)
in goggles and his leather hat
with ears just poking out like that—
Flying reckless, looking smug
searching for a juicy bug

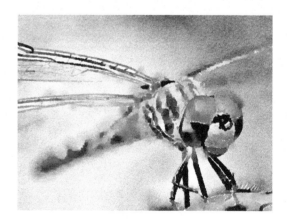

For that's why bilbies often fly
To catch fat bugs up in the sky—
Once while chasing bugs in Spain
he found a hornet on the plain
Who warned the bilby "stay away!"
But Filby ate him anyway!

In China there were bad bugs too
like dragonflies "The Brothers Foo"
Who tried to bring the bilby down
by swarming round him upside down—

Today you'd search the whole land through
and never find "The Brothers Foo"!

Worst of all, "Les Bees" of France
who led him in a skyward dance—
Rolls and loops and spirals round
they tried to crash him to the ground—
They battled there from dusk to dawn
but now "Les Bees" are VERY gone!

After eating bugs in France
and Timbuktu and old Murmansk—
Hardly one fat moth remained
from California to Fort Wayne

Parliament passed a special bill
A special "Filby Bilby Bill" [22I]
To honor one who heard the call
and ate the bugs of city hall

Maybe you've looked to the sky
and seen a bilby flying by—
Looping inside, upside down
turning circles round and round

Or maybe you've just been surprised
to look into the pilot's eyes
and see he's not a man at all—
But just a small marsupial!

And most Australians know by sight
this little creature of the night—
That eats fat bugs and crawly things
and creepy insects having wings—

Whose favorite sport is flying round
far above the night time ground—
For NOW Australians can explain
why Filby Bilby flies his plane

Filby Bilby's still a star
but doesn't drive a fancy car
or fly the fastest aeroplane
from Adelaide to northern Spain

And if you asked him why he stayed
just west of Perth in Wally's Glade—   [
His eyes would gaze so far away
and voice would hush, as he would say:

"Although I've toured the USA
And ate the moths of Mandalay
and tasty flies of Budapest—
Australian bugs are still the best!"

THE END

Firefly Frog

Firefly frog
Lived in the bog
Perched on a log
Shrouded in fog

Quiet and sly
Not knowing why
Wanted to try
Snatch firefly

During the day
All work; no play
Froggy would stay
Waiting for prey

But in the night
Feasting just right
Made quite a sight
His tummy would light

Flip-Flop

Mother
Brother
Sister
POP!

Kitten
Puppy
Bunny
HOP!

Upside
Downside
Bottom
TOP!

Green light
Blue light
Red light
STOP!

Gracie Gopher

Lazy sunshine
Gracie Gopher
Not a worker
Just a loafer

Digging gophers
Dug the ground
But Gracie yearned
To lay around

Hungry gophers
Chewed the hay
Gracie dozed
Through the day

Summer ended
Fall was here
Hibernation
Time was near

Worried gophers
Told her straight.
"Gracie dear
It's getting late!"

Autumn wind
Began to blow
Gophers scurried
To and fro

Gracie yawned
Closed her eyes.
Time remained
She surmised

Sleepy gophers
Went below
But Gracie had
Nowhere to go

Found a hole
From the storm
Somewhat dry
Not too warm

Bitter winter
Shivering
Gracie said
"I'll work next spring!"

Blessed Ones

Jesus blessed
the little ones
baby daughters
infant sons
cherub spirits
gentle doves
ours to cherish
God's to love

Herbert Hippopotamus

Sunning by the river side
with a body extra-wide
Wet and sour grumpy-puss
Herbert Hippopotamus

Giant mouth opens W-I-D-E!
Would you like to look inside?
Sure you would, it's like a door–
Just to hear his awful ROAR!

See his mammoth toothy grin
You could almost climb right in
No, you say – And just why not?
Does his breath smell bad a lot?

You must tell him (make a fuss)
Listen, hippopotamus
May I have just one small wish?
Your breath it smells like rotten fish!
You don't eat fish? No-no you say?
You just eat grass and weeds and hay?
I hope you don't just kiss and tell–
With breath like rotten fishy smell

Perhaps you should eat extra mush
Or better yet, just floss and brush!
So, open up! Please open wide–
That I may look around inside
To brush your teeth both up and down
and those in front, around and round

HOLY COW! There's so much room!
To brush these teeth, I'd need a broom!
And giant tubes of "Hippo Mint"
(that tastes a lot like dryer lint)

So here's a question just for you
as you consider what to do–
Who lays along the river side
and often underwater hides
with open mouth so clean and W-I-D-E
So clean, you might just climb inside?

You're right! You're right to guess as much–
IT'S HERBERT HIPPOPOTAMUS!

Dear Mr. LaBubba,
A gnome in good standing, I've heard much about...
So could you, good gnome, dear Mr. LaBubba
address other gnomes in Flubba Dee-Dubba
and ask they remove sharp needles and pins...
Sincerely,
Santa Claus

Hubba LaBubba

Early one morning in Flubba Dee-Dubba
in the home of a gnome, Mr. Hubba LaBubba
there arrived in the mail a most curious note–
delivered by pigeon or wigeon or goat

The note was from Santa, you know, Mr. Claus
who mailed it to Hubba LaBubba because
gnomes hereabouts were grouchy old grouches
and Santa sliding down chimneys got ouches
from needles and nettles and sharp-pointed pins
placed to keep Santa Claus out and not in–
so children could be such bad little grouches
and Santa not leave their presents on couches
or anywhere else in Flubba Dee-Dubba–
and that's why Santa wrote Hubba LaBubba.

Dear Mr. LaBubba, the note started out
*A gnome in good standing, I've heard much about
from many fine helpers who stock up my shelves
the wisest and oldest of all Santa's elves
who say you keep Christmas with holiday joy
and give happy goodies to each girl and boy*

*So could you, good gnome, dear Mr. LaBubba
address other gnomes in Flubba Dee-Dubba
and ask they remove sharp needles and pins
so Santa might leave their presents within
for little gnome children on pillows and couches
and stop them from being such bad little grouches?*

So Hubba LaBubba sat down on a stool
considering Flubbian's first golden rule–
*No smiling or grinning or laughing in town
For Flubbian children must wear only frowns!*

Then Hubba LaBubba remembering Christmas
and birthdays and parties and clowns in the circus–
before being grouchy had saddened the clowns
before being grouchy made Flubbians frown

Then Hubba LaBubba jumped up from his place
and ran through the door with a smile on his face
out into the street and through all the shops
with giggles and wiggles and hoppity-hops
He sang to the barber and grocer and tailor
and lawyer and blacksmith and saltwater sailor!
And after the gnome had covered a mile–
each gnome he had touched was wearing a smile!

Dear Hubba LaBubba,
MERRY CHRISTMAS!
Sincerely,
Santa Claus

Gnomes hopped and skipped and danced in the streets
they jiggled and squiggled and wiggled their feets
and soon all the town was as glad as could be–
so they marched to the square and trimmed up a tree
With bobbles and tinsel and bright colored lights
the Flubbian town glowed bright in the night

But Flubbians frowned as they started to leave
Tomorrow was Christmas, tonight Christmas eve
Santa would miss them, fly past in the night–
Time was so short, there was no time to write!

Hubba LaBubba was sad as could be
as he placed an angel on top of the tree—
Then over the land the darkness did creep
and Flubbian children fell fastest asleep

Around about midnight, Santa flew past
his sleigh painted red, his reindeer so fast
and seeing the town aglow in the light
landed in Flubba on Christmas eve night
To give happy presents to good little gnomes
like a truck or a doll or a brush or a comb

And early next morning in Flubba Dee-Dubba
in the home of a gnome, Mr. Hubba LaBubba
A curious sound rose up from the streets
of laughing and playing and stomping of feets
The singing and dancing of each girl and boy–
Good Flubbian gnomes were singing with joy!
And hung on the hearth right next to his tree
a note on a paper as plain as could be:

Dear Mr. LaBubba, the note started out–
A gnome in good standing, I hadn't a doubt.
I'm writing to tell you the chimneys were bare
the needles were missing, the nettles weren't there
Sharp pins didn't poke me, I didn't get "ouches"
So Santa left oodles of presents on couches
and everywhere else in Flubba Dee-Dubba–

MERRY CHRISTMAS TO YOU, DEAR HUBBA LABUBBA!

The Kite

Dance on air
Bright sunlight
Tree and meadow
Magic flight

Paper fellow
Grandest sight
Wisps of wind
Hold on tight!

Ladybug

Ladybug, ladybug what do you see
Perched at the top of the Sycamore tree
Sipping aphid soup and spider mite tea
From cups of Pistachio shells

Ladybug, ladybug, come fly with me
To travel the world in extravagancy
And take our swims in the best Chablis
At the finest grand hotels

Ladybug, ladybug, come marry me
And furnish our nest so elegantly
In a cozy spot in the old settee
On a musty porch in the dell

Ladybug, ladybug what do you see
Perched at the top of the Sycamore tree
Do you see our children one, two, three
Climbing on the old church bell?

Ladybug, ladybug, come dance with me
On our silver wedding jubilee
And toast our love with spider mite tea
From cups of Pistachio shells

Library Lion

Library Lion was always trying
to be a good King of Beasts
But that trying left him crying
He wasn't a beast in the least!

It takes more than claws
to uphold the laws
of jungle and African plain
For passing laws (for jaws and paws)
Requires a mane *and* a brain!

Take for example, as only a sample
the problems elephants made
An ample example, elephants trample
around in the shade of the glade

Elephants crashing, rudely splashing
in waters where crocodiles laid
Library listened to both positions
Then ruled the elephants WADE!

Library agreed, antelope need
to huddle together in bunches
Heed their need to feed with speed
or they could end up as lunches!

Library was wary, quite contrary
of animals acting crude
Took a look in his etiquette book
to find their behavior was rude!

Library Lion was always trying
to make the right sort of ruling
And find a way to make his play
for reading, writing, and schooling

Library at least is still King of Beasts
but doubles as "Monarch of Fineness"
And spends his day ruling away
a jungle filled with kindness

So, if today is not going your way
and you feel the need to tussle
Take a look in Library's book
Use your brain instead of muscle!

THE LUNCH BOX POEMS

Louise

There's a spider
in my lunchbox—
I think it is
Louise

There's a spider
in my lunchbox—
she is napping
on my cheese!

Just before
our spelling test
I went to get
a snack

Louise
was sipping
apple juice
lying
on her back!

I went to eat
an orange
before we
started math

Louise was
in my thermos
getting ready
for a bath!

What about
the kids
who see
a spider
in my soup?

What am I
supposed
to say
to such a
nosy group?

What about
the kids
who see
a spider
in my lunch?

What am I
supposed
to say
to such a
nosey bunch?

Oh no!
It's almost
lunchtime—
I'm scared
to lift the latch
I hope she
doesn't
run away—
Louise is hard
to catch

I listen
very closely
but cannot hear
a peep

Perhaps Louise
is in the
peanut butter
fast asleep!

Perhaps I'm not
so hungry—
I'll have some
milk instead

or maybe
she's not
there at all—
but simply
in my head

Lunchbox Beetle

There's a beetle in my lunchbox
I think his name is Ned
He burrowed in my sandwich
And put himself to bed

He made himself a pillow
From the soft PB and J
Then pulled the crust up over him
And that is where he lay

My bestest friend is Theodore
We often trade our lunch
Today he ate my Beetlewich
Until he felt a CRUNCH

I felt a whole lot sorry
For my little beetle Ned
Cause being in a tummy
Is not the bestest bed

Wilberforce

There's a horsefly
in my lunchbox—
It must be
Wilberforce

Why is he
on my sandwich
instead of on
his horse?

Why is he
on my cupcake
and oatmeal
cookie too?

He had go to
school today
but he had
the flu

Why is he
on my pudding
and in my
cottage cheese?

Why is he
in my thermos?
OH NO!
I heard him
SNEEZE!

It's not polite
to holler—
In school
you shouldn't
scream

But if I didn't
stop him
he'd get my
chocolate cream!

I opened up
my lunchbox
and shouted out
in force

"Wilberforce
you go home
and get back
on your HORSE!"

The Shoeful Shrew

I opened my eyes
and jumped out of bed
woke up my brother
and whispering said—

"Willie, wake up
and see what I do—
Just look over there
THERE'S A SHREW IN MY SHOE!"

Sure enough on the floor
in my shoe by the chair
was a little pink nose
stuck up in the air!

"THERE'S A SHREW IN YOUR SHOE"
he said with surprise—
"And a mean one at that
by the look in his eyes!"

"You must get him out
don't let him stay there—
He'll soon make a nest
out of kangaroo hair!"

The shrew ducked inside
when I picked up the shoe
and shook it around
to shake out the shrew

He wouldn't come out
when I shook the shoe so
being real late for school
I decided to go!

There wasn't a choice
shrew or no shrew
so I sat on the bed
and put on my shoe!

It was good that my mother
had bought me big shoes—
"Your feet are still growing
and these are size twos!"

I ran for the bus
first uphill then down
and each time I stepped
the shrew bounced around!

When I got on the bus
the bus driver said—
"I looked at your feet
and saw a small head!"

I had to think fast
for everyone knew
that stuck in my shoe
was a stowaway shrew!

"How nice you all noticed
the shrew in my shoe—
I taught him to stay there
and dance just for you!"

I sat in my seat
with my foot in the aisle—
Till out popped the shrew
with a big friendly smile

"Mississippi," I said
for that was his name—
"Dance for the children—
You see, he's so tame!"

Tippity-tappity
eekity-squeak—
The shrew danced a dance
like he practiced a week

The other kids wondered
how such a fine shrew
could ever have learned
to dance on my shoe

The classroom was crowded
with children who came—
To see Mississippi
dance just the same

Ms. Wiggle, my teacher
was very impressed—
She said, "Mississippi
you sure are the best!"

So I spent the whole day
autographing their books
as children dropped by
my class for a look

At the shrew in my shoe
with his nose poking out
asleep on the laces
and all tired out

So if one fine day
you jump out of bed
to find in your shoe
a small shrew instead

Just give him a pillow
and small fuzzy quilt
a worm for his breakfast
and warm glass of milk

Do NOT wake your brother
for what you should do—
Is go to your closet
and wear different shoes!

Mole Splash Soupé

There's a mole in my soup
It's an awful disgrace–
And making things worse
There's a smile on his face!

I told the lunch lady–
Hey just look at him!
What's the problem? She asked–
He's just taking his swim

Eight laps round the bowl
He swims every day–
Dries off with a towel
and goes on his way

Then lays in the sun
or goes for a jog
or sits in the sauna
or tramps in the bog

Tomorrow's the same
it's sort of a loop–
He'll end up back here
for a swim in my soup!

He thinks it's a place
like the YMCA–
He thinks it's a place
he can swim every day!

He's blind as a bat
so he swims in my soup–
But I haven't the heart
to tell him the truth

So we make up our soup
before he comes in
and he sits on the edge
of the bowl on the rim

And takes off his shoes
and puts his toes in–
Then he swims and he swims
And he swims and he swims!

Each day I come back
for soup by the bowl
and sit in my seat
and wait for the mole

To take off his shoes
as he sits on the rim
and works up his courage
to finally jump in!

And when he is finished
and goes on his way
I eat my lunch cold–
My Mole Splash Soupé!

THE END

Picklepillar

There is a garden spot distiller
Called the busy Picklepillar
Twenty legs and eyes like dots
Black and orange leopard spots

Caterpillar full of knowledge
Graduate of Pickle College
Picks cucumbers off the ground
Only when they're fat and round

Not too big and not too ripe
Sort them out by size and type
Throws them in a great big pot
Heats the water boiling hot

Twenty legs are quite a bunch
Stirring up his pickle punch
People picklers can take months
But he can do five jobs at once!

Cooks them up so soft and nice
Adds a dash of pickle spice
Stuffs them in the jar just right
Twists the lid on extra tight!

Displays the jars for all to see
Advertises on TV
Pickle lovers are his target
Super-Dillers in the market

Beneath a garden canopy [42A]
In a place that's hard to see
Picklepillar sells his wares
To skunks and hares and grizzly bears

To those of you who think contrary
And think his pickles ordinary—
Try a jar of Super-Dillers
From a store named Picklepillar's!

Messy Puppy

Puppy is wet
And puppy is smelly
wet on her back
and wet on her belly

wet on her whiskers
and wet on her nose
mud on her tummy
and mud on her toes

mud on her ears
and mud on her knees
mud from a puddle
thick as you please

puppy shakes water
soaks all my clothes
starts at her tail
and ends at her nose

my puppy is sleepy
curled on the rug
quiet now – SHHHH
give my puppy a hug

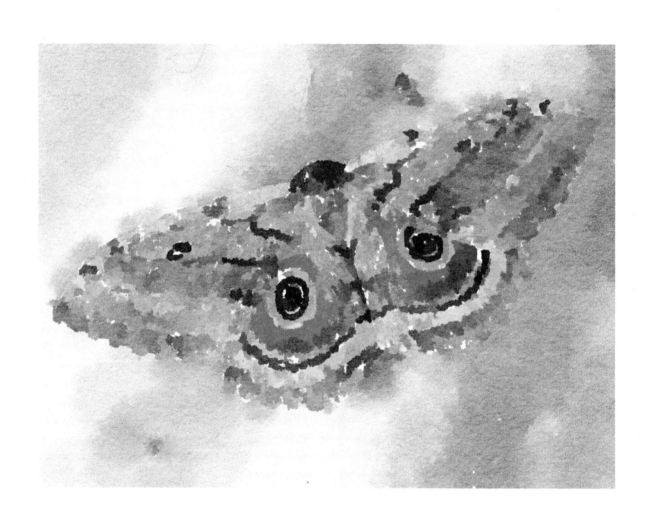

Fuzzy Speckled Moth

Changing slowly, I evolved
from caterpillar and cocoon
to timid fuzzy speckled moth
who hid by day and flew at night
when it was absolutely safe

"Don't touch my wings!" I reproached
"The dust of life, which lets me fly
with soaring lift, will surely fade
and I will fall to earth again"

As caterpillars both, my friend
we built cocoons and lived within
and grew to moths of varied hue–

Then we flew, and touched our wings
and shared our dust on starry nights

And when I cried in mortal dread
You said, but never understood–
"Fuzzy speckles are your bane!
They only add to clumsiness–
Hide them, hide them underneath
or you will never ride the wind!"

Those fuzzy speckles were unique
they set me out from other moths
and gave me cause and exposé
to better understand my heart

A fuzzy speckled moth remains
but one no longer fearing flight
or worried so about his dust–

One who bravely soars aloft
and cries aloud in lilting song–
To seek a grander elegance
on fuzzy wings and gentle wind

Izzy

I took my dog down to the show
To see if she could win
But when we got up to the door
They wouldn't let us in

Does your dog have papers?
The man asked with a shout
I said we put some on the floor
But now we let her out

I'm mean is she a pure bred
Her parents duly logged?
Yes, I'm really pretty sure
Her mom and dad were dogs

I mean is she a Redbone
Or Bluetick hunting hound?
No, I do not think so
She's only black and brown

I'm sorry son, the show is closed
To dogs with no blood lines—
Once she did step on a nail
But now her paw is fine

Listen son, she can't come in
She has no pedigree—
No, Izzy didn't go to school
But does read books with me

She lies beside me every night
Before I go to bed
And listens to my problems
And every word I've said

See, Izzy is my bestest friend
And guards me every day
To keep the ugly monsters out
And chase my fears away

That's why Izzy came today
I know that she can win—
But the man just slammed the door
And did not let us in

I hope the dog that finally wins
Is someone's bestest friend
Cause really that's the only thing
That matters in the end

NASA

They say NASA's a place
where science gets done
like sending off rocket ships
toward the moon and the sun

But I'm not so sure
(cause the sun's awfully hot)
and rockets might burn up
right there on the spot

But they go up to moon
they've done that a bunch
and picked up some rocks
but then left after lunch

I do not understand
why they do not go back
Perhaps it's because
Someone's taken their map

NASA, let's see—
just what could it mean?
Is it some fancy building
or flying machine?

Does it mean something special
Like National Splat?
No, that word's too big
and won't fit on a hat

I can't figure it out
Just what NASA means
But maybe that's better
I'm only thirteen

I just don't believe
they get too much done
blasting off rockets
to the moon or the sun

or faraway places
like Kalamazoo—
but simply a name
to fool me and you

Nat E. Newt

Old dismal place
Dark secret space
Skin grooved as lace
Shy reptile face

Nat E. Newt
Hidden under root
Wouldn't say cute
Scaly birthday suit

Color reddish-gray
Inside to stay
Never got to play
In light of day

At day's close
Others might doze
Natty (I suppose)
Wears business clothes

Roams all night
Moon's pale light
Makes quite a sight
Dressed just right

Cool night air
Trading in wares
Wares sold in pairs
Nat seldom cares

Surely told
Bargains bold
Dealings cold
Bought and sold

Nat E. Newt
Never was cute
Or too astute
Wearing a suit

Sunrise grace
Clothing erase
Tired Newt face
Finds sleepy place

Pica Mawah

In the Susquehatan village, where the Seven Waters narrow
Lived a boy named Pica Mawah, son of warrior Magua Saro.
Born of mother, Yukiwatan, seven snowy winters past
Of his family's seven children, Pica Mawah was the last.

Moccasins of toughened deerskin, softest breeches, woven blouse
Playing games with other children; hide-and-seek; fox-catch-mouse.
Make believing they were hunters; tracking deer and stalking bear
Who could shoot the farthest arrow high into the frigid air?

Pica Mawah and his pony, Shico Lupo (chestnut mane)
Learned to track woodland creatures in the snow and misty rain.
Another friend, wolf cub Charo, followed closely by his side
Trailing little Pica Mawah everywhere the boy would ride.

After dark, children gathered in their cozy fire lit home
Listened to the oldest stories as the smoke curled to the dome.
Father told of Askachubo, greatest bear of Lenape Forest
Goddess of the hunt incarnate, guide of ancient warriors past.

Pica longed to be a warrior, wear the honored blouse of yellow
And mounted tall on Shico Lupo, ride by father Magua Saro.
He would stalk the fiercest grizzly, face the danger all alone
Shoot an arrow; strike the grizzly; pierce his heart; shatter bone.

The glowing fire on father's face projected such an eerie light
A mystical and spirit presence fell upon the lodge that night.
As Pica Mawah fell to slumber, shadows danced along the wall
Mighty mystic ancient warriors summoned him with echoed call.

Early on the hunting morning, sun shone bright upon the hill
Pica Mawah woke excited, perhaps today he'd prove his skill.
Mother worked preparing cornmeal for the family's noon repast
The corn she baked would be nutritious, but she knew it was the last.

"Father, father" Pica asked him, "May I join the hunt today?"
"Not today my little Pica. The trip will take us far away.
Stay at home with Yukiwatan. The lodge you must keep safe and warm.
There is danger in the heavens; clouds foretell a winter storm."

Village elders knew of hunger in the coldest winter months
Survival of the village people rested on successful hunts.
Warriors of tested prowess ventured forth in search of game
Weathering the greatest hardship seeking legendary fame.

Hunting warriors on their ponies left the village to the east
Followed by the mournful chanting of the elder tribal priest.
Pica standing by his mother, watched the party go their way
Saw a tear fall on her bosom as she turned and faced away.

"Mother," Pica asked politely, "Will our father come back soon?"
"Yes, my little Pica-chito, with the next bright hunter's moon."
Pica Mawah's oldest sister, Sastowaka (child first born)
Called to Pica quite abruptly, "Help us with the breakfast corn!"

Helping serve the village elders, those too old to leave the nest
Pica saw the winter storm was quickly building in the west.
As the sky turned darkest gray, winter's wind began to ring
Pica Mawah, in the distance, heard the Askachubo sing.

Putting on his warmest deerskin, fur-lined boots, and woven gown
Mounted on his Shico Lupo, snow was falling lightly down.
The hunting party tracks were fading, trees were bending in the wind
Calling Charo, grey-wolf brother, their fateful trip would soon begin.

The storm was growing stronger now; the trail it seemed to swallow
Pica Mawah searching for a path the group could safely follow.
Shico Lupo struggled onward, deepest snow up to his chest
Pica Mawah pushed them forward; forward on their ancient quest.

Suddenly the storm had slackened, winter wind began to slow
And standing tall before the hunter was the mystic Askachubo.
Time stood still for bear and hunter, neither noticed snow or ice
Askachubo seemed to offer up himself as a sacrifice.

Pica Mawah knew the scripted role that he must play
Though he felt an admiration for the ancient bear that day.
He drew an arrow from his quiver, placed it tautly on the bow
Drew the bowstring to his cheek and smoothly let it go.

The arrow rushed through tree and bushes hardly making any sound
Slashed into the great bear's heart, striking Askachubo down.
The great beast lurched and fell face forward; snow around him bloody red
Then Pica saw the phantom goddess, as the ancient legend said.

The goddess Askachubo gestured, turned and seemed to float away
Pica Mawah and his party followed her throughout the day.
Shico Lupo bore the lifeless bear upon her back
Pica and his grey-wolf Charo pushed along the snowy track.

As shadows fell and daylight waned, the party found a cave
Then the goddess Askachubo vanished in a misty haze.
Pica Mawah built a fire in the cave to keep them warm
Outside raged the wind and fury of the bitter winter storm.

Through the night and all the day, it snowed without a sound
But Pica Mawah and his friends were warm beneath the ground.
They drank the water from the snow and huddled in their den.
Shico Lupo ate the leaves of trees found growing near the glen.

Meanwhile back inside the village, people were concerned
Without the boy, Pica Mawah's father had returned.
Then his mother, Yukiwatan and father, Magua Saro
Rode their ponies toward the place where Seven Waters narrow.

The woods were snowy, dark and deep, a trail could not be found
Then suddenly a brilliant light seemed to hover near the ground.
The searchers unbelieving saw a phantom to their front
Incarnate now in great bear form, the goddess of the hunt!

The great beast turned and loped away, the searchers close behind
She led them through the deepest woods, a place they would not find.
The great bear stopped and stood erect then motioned as a wave
And moved away to show the searchers entrance to a cave.

People from the village came to cheer and some to stare
And give a hero's welcome to Pica Mawah and his bear.
All the village elders came to praise (and some to brood)
The bravest little village boy who brought them so much food.

When the hunting party left next dawn to hunt some game
Warriors of tested prowess searching lasting fame.
With them Pica Mawah rode close by Magua Saro
With Shico Lupo, grey wolf Charo, and a blouse of yellow

In years to come, Pica Mawah often rode alone
With Shico Lupo, grey-wolf Charo, traveled far from home.
Then in a solemn secret place, the warrior found a glade
And to the goddess of the wood, most devoutly prayed.

And sometimes in the evening light, when sunset cast its glow
The warrior called the phantom forth of goddess Askachubo.
As silence fell upon the wood, the giant bear would come
And man and beast in stillness stood and soon became as one.

Previc of Perth

Previc of Perth was a dragon by birth
Whose pants were a size eighty-four
And a body so large he moved like a barge
On feet as big as a door

Strange it may seem a dragon would dream
Of being a knight on a horse
A reptile in armor he'd be such a charmer
And rescue a maiden of course!

Previc was lonely and dreaming the only
Thing that made him feel good
For most people cried when they saw him outside
And ran away to the wood!

Now a maiden in Perth was a beauty at birth
A lovelier girl never was
And right from the start she won Previc's heart
But kept it a secret because

Folks thought that dragons were bad scallywaggins
Who terrorized city and farm
And used burning breath scaring people to death
Causing nothing but trouble and harm

Fair Maiden of Perth knew in spite of his birth
Previc had good in his heart
And soon found a way to send him each day
A freshly baked raspberry tart

It made the girl sad that others were glad
When into their town rode a knight
Gallant Sir Faust who had come from a joust
Was seeking a dragon to fight!

"Previc of Perth, you scoundrel from birth
Come out and fight this brave knight!
So I can be savin' the loveliest maiden
Surrender you dragon or fight!"

The crowd gave a shout when Previc stepped out
And stood alone in the dale
The scallywag dragon a sword he was draggin'
And armored from head to his tail!

So what would you think if you stood on the brink
Of fighting a dragon so large
With feet like a door and sized eighty-four
And a body as big as a barge?

You probably would skid as Faust nearly did
When he stopped his horse in the charge
And stood there in awe as he looked up and saw
A dragon-knight scaly and large!

"Sir Previc of Perth, of fine dragon birth"
He said acting nervous and glum—
"It's not really right to dress like a knight
You made me swallow my gum!"

The Maiden of Perth for all she was worth
Kissed the fair dragon-turned-knight
The big dragon blushed and when the crowd hushed
It signaled the end of the fight!

Sir Faust rode away at the end of the day
With a story no one would believe
To tell of a dragon whose big tail was draggin'
The maiden he just couldn't leave!

So when you're in Perth near the edge of the earth
You'll find the folks having fun
And families of dragons with little tongues waggin'
For raspberry tarts in the sun!

Santa Claus

If Santa Claus is on his way
Does he really come by sleigh?
Or would he fly an aero plane
Above the snow and wind and rain?

Or maybe he would take a boat
To keep his many toys afloat
Across the ocean to the bay
Do you think he comes that way?

Perhaps he's on the way right now
I hope his sleigh has got a plow
Because the snow is falling fast
To cover roads and trees and grass

Will he need a place to park?
Our big back yard is very dark
And sure would be some lousy luck
If Santa and his sleigh got stuck

Then he'd have to spend the night
And we would talk until daylight
And have some milk and cookies too—
But the reindeer have to stay in the garage

Shoes

What do fluffy bunnies wear?
Hip shoes! Hop shoes!
What do shaggy ponies wear?
Clip shoes! Clop shoes!
What do swimming fishes wear?
Drip shoes! Drop shoes!
What do cuddly ducklings wear?
Flip shoes! Flop shoes!

Whose shoes are the biggest shoes?
Whale shoes! Whale shoes!
Whose shoes are the smallest shoes?
Ant shoes! Ant shoes!
Whose shoes are the muddy shoes?
Pig shoes! Pig shoes!
Whose shoes are the pretty shoes?
My shoes! My shoes!

Snackosaurs

Little Loren went to sleep
Dreaming of delicious treats
Craving pre-historic sweets
Snacks that cave-boys used to eat

Not since long before his birth
Dinosaurs had walked the earth
In a cave with rocky floors
Searching for the *Snackosaurs*

Snackosaurs were yummy beasts
Making dandy cave-boy feasts
Lived a zillion years ago
Hungry cave-boys ought to know

A flying snack was quite the sight
Its name was *Candyappledite*
With wings as big as aeroplanes
He made his nest from candy canes

Tri-choclat-drops (a favorite treat)
Lived high on Peanut Butter Peak
As winter chill made dinos shiver
Cocoa swam in Hot Fudge River

A most ferocious beast was next
His name was *Tacosaurus Mex*
With razor teeth and giant jaws
He made tacos with his claws

One last creature to devour
A most delicious *Gummy-sour*
Set apart from others duller
Gummies came in rainbow colors

Snackosaurs were fun to eat
Extra-special cave boy treats
Tri-choclat-drops were soft and gooey
Gummy-sours were rather chewy

Cave-Dad soon addressed the bunch
No Snackosaurs 'til after lunch
Loren woke and yelled *Whoopee*
Cave-boys were a lot like me!

Sneezy Bunny

There was a bunny rabbit
with a sneezy sort of habit
bunny rabbit with a habit
a peculiar kind of rabbit

Dusty pollen from the trees
in the very slightest breeze
made him itch, cough and wheeze
and eventually to sneeze

He sneezed and he wheezed
from the pollen in the trees
Sneezy trees full of bees
making honey in the breeze

So he called up Doctor Mink
who conjured up a drink
using honey colored pink
that he mixed up in his sink

Mink's honey tasted sunny
to a sneezing wheezy bunny
then his nose wasn't runny—
He was just a normal bunny!

Snuggles

I hug my Snuggles every day
just to say - I care
and pat his nose and rub his ears
and ruffle up his hair—
I take him from his cozy shelf
so we can go outside
and put him on my bicycle[16A]
and take him for a ride—
I peddle round to grandma's house
it's down around the block
and park my bike and run inside
it's nearly nine o'clock!

My grandma seems so awfully glad
to see my "Snuggles Bear"
because her kisses kind of leave
some wet spots on his hair
and then she says "Good Morning Bear"
and holds him on her gown
and gives us both a squeezy hug
before she puts him down [49]
I don't know what she'd ever do
without my Bear and I
to help her eat those cookies
and that huckleberry pie

I bet if Snuggles missed a day
or stayed up on the shelf
my grandma would be so sad
to eat that pie herself

Space Frog

I think I have a frog from space
like Mercury or some such place—
Whose rocket ship had spun about
and this poor frog had fallen out

A frog that looked a bit surprised
with bumpy skin and bulging eyes
and kind of green and sort of large
who landed THUMP by our garage

He spoke in whispers very low
(and knew most everything to know)
and raised his head up to announce
RUMPY-GRUMPY-BUMPY-BOUNCE

I studied him for quite a spell
to learn what secrets he could tell
about his life on distant moons
and frolicking on lunar dunes
or spinning tales of Saturn's rings
of princely frogs or frogly kings

Of blasting off to deepest space
to ancient times and ancient place
or tell of now (or now and then)
of how or why (or where and when)

Am-phi-bian propelled through time
beyond a place that doesn't rhyme—
Far beyond the twinkling stars
past the moon and WAY past Mars

But I was haunted by his words
(BUMPY-BOUNCE seemed so absurd)
and searched and searched for many days
to find someone who knew his ways

To learn the secret RUMPY-BUMP
and why he landed with a thump
to grace the grass by our garage
all kind of green and sort of large

I asked our mailman with a smile
if he could linger for a while
to understand my frog from space
but said he had no time to waste
on such a "fat and ugly toad"
and hurried off along the road

I asked the janitor from school
if he could tell my frog was cool
but he just swept across the room
and tried to smush him with a broom

I'm still not sure if I was mad
(or only really, really sad)
and didn't know what next to do
to find that very special clue
which made him secretly announce
RUMPY-GRUMPY-BUMPY-BOUNCE

I sat alone by our garage
(with my frog so green and large)
until the cold and dripping snout
of Rose, my dog, soon poked about

Rose stood high above the frog
(she looked like any other dog)
then raised her head up to announce
RUMPY-GRUMPY-BUMPY-BOUNCE

Instantly the frog had jumped
way up high on Rosie's rump
and dog and frog bumped out of sight
around the corner to the right

I couldn't yell or even speak
(I just felt weird and kind of weak)
but then my mind began to race—
I think I have a DOG FROM SPACE!

Tugboat Tessie

Tessie pulls and pushes
The big ships away
From their harbor moorings
Far out in the bay

Tessie revved her engine
Hard against the spray
Poop! Poop! Said the tugboat
Stay clear of my way!

One night it was foggy
Waves the ocean tossed
And little Tessie worried
A big ship might get lost

A search light struggled
To shine through the mist
Boop! Boop! Yelled a big ship
I'm starting fast to list!

Tessie snugly moored
To her berth at the dock
Heard the call to tugboats
Big ship near the rocks!

Tessie raced up her engine
Speeding toward the scene
Poop! Poop! Said the tugboat
I'm a pushing' machine!

The big ship struggled
To stay off the reef
Until Tessie chugged up
On his bow like a thief

Bump! Thump! Was the sound
As Tessie rammed the boat
She must get there quickly
So the ship would stay afloat

It took most of her strength
To push the ship away
And guide him back safely
To his mooring in the bay

All the big ships tooted
Well done! The ships did say
Poop! Poop! Answered Tessie
It's just the tugboat way!

The Ballad of Mallard Drake

Way down south were the time is slow
Way done south were the cowboys go
With the sun so hot that buffaloes bake
Was an ugly varmint called Mallard Drake

Drake was a duck and a mean one too
With a Colt 45 and a snake tattoo
A beak so tough he ground up nails
And breath so foul it'd leave you pale

A duck with a gun is a scary sight
A duck with a gun in the pale moonlight
Drake came to town on a hurtin' spree—
And part a that spree was a hurtin' me

A duck with a badge, we ain't but a few
And on this night I'd a job to do
Cause a law duck's life is a deadly game
Chasin' varmints in the snow and rain

Such was the case that stormy night
As I stood there waitin for a big gunfight
I was facin a critter I knew too well
But oh my Lord that duck did smell

He smelled so bad the mosquitoes died
Gallopin' horses fainted mid-stride
Stores exploded and bars burned down
There wasn't a soul left around that town

Then Drake made a move for that 45
I had to be fast just to stay alive
But I kept that duck from a hangman's rope
When I drew from my holster –
A bar of soap

I threw 'em in a tub and lathered his wings
He started to smell like the sweetest thing
And after he'd soaked in that tub a while
The ugly old varmint just a started to smile

He threw down his gun and wrung out his shirt
As all that mean washed away with the dirt
Now you might say it was a bit of odd luck
But whatever it was—
He became a new duck

Now way down south where the time is slow
Way down south where the cowboys go
Is a beauty salon called "The Sweet Shampoo"
With a Mallard duck owner—
But I won't say who

Tippy T. Toad

Tippy T. Toad sat near the road
In a garden of carrots and peas
Crouched in a bunch, she waited for lunch
Delectable beetles or fleas

Tippy T. Toad was stuck in a mode
Uncommon for one of her kind
Lacking the zeal to leave for a meal
She feared to go outside and dine

Tippy T. Toad knew a beetle or two
Was the diet of choice for a toad
But had not the verve or even the nerve
So most of her food she had stowed

Tippy T. Toad played in the shade
And heard a small voice from behind
"Hello, young toad perched by the road
Come out in the morning sunshine!"

Gaining support from her unseen cohort
Tippy Toad crawled from her place
Slowly at first then one rapid burst
The toad felt sun on her face

"Hurray!" said the voice, "You've made a fine choice!
Reached for your place in the sun"
Indeed the young toad felt free of her load
Being out in the sun was such fun

"Who are you my chum?" Asked toad with a hum
Of course she was naturally shy
That is, of course, till she spotted the source
Came from an articulate fly

The fly stood up proud and shouted out loud
"Are you thankful?" he asked as a hunch
"I am," said the toad as she lunged from the road
And ate the poor fly for her lunch

Clayton Toad

Clayton Toad beside the road
eyed the other side–
But the road, thought the toad
looked so *big* and wide!

Bugs, he thought, could be caught
much quicker over there–
Where they sat, round and fat
delicious insect fare!

Bikes, trikes and motorcykes
careened along the road–
Crazy ducks driving trucks
never even slowed!

Clayton asked a bird for word
of how she crossed the pike–
"I fly up high across the sky
and land just where I like!"

So he spread his chubby arms
flapped with all his might–
But try and try, he could not fly
to any sort of height!

He watched a snake calmly make
a dash and then a rush–
Out of luck (the snake was struck)
and smushed into a mush

Then the toad beside the road
saw on the other side–
A spotted frog beside a log
eyes opened big and wide

"Hey Mr. Frog beside the log"
Clayton called across–
"I must say that today
you look a little lost!"
"I'm not lost," the frog replied
"Only deep in thought"
"Bugs on *your* side fat and wide
and begging to be caught!"

Then Clayton realized the truth
about that road so wide–
Half of all the insect world
was on *his* very side!

So when you think another place
is better than your own–
Realize there's nowhere else
as wonderful as home!

- 175 -

Wally Giggles

Wally Worm could really wiggle
(I mean really, really jiggle)
In the morning he would shiver
and his body start to quiver

Wally Worm was feeling icky
and his body kind of sticky–
When his tummy did a squiggle
making Wally squirm and giggle!

Wally's brother, Willie Worm
soon began to twist and turn–
Giggle-wiggle round and round
over-under-upside down

That is how their day would go
as they wiggled high and low–
Squiggle up - jiggle down
giggle silly - wiggle round!

Being giggly soon caught on
(it affected Stanley Swan)
as he floated on the pond–
Ducks and geese just giggled on!

Silly giggles passed to Snork
cultured gopher from New York
eating salad with a fork–
Passed his giggle to a stork

Sally Stork sent babies big-gle
to a hog and then a pig-gle–
Everyone a piggle-wiggle
soon the barnyard was a-giggle!

Farmer Jones and Mrs. Brown
giggled all the way to town
passing chuckles all around–
Gave their giggles to a hound

Billy Beagle feeling rotten
put the giggle in some cotton
there it stayed almost forgotten–
Know who lived inside the cotton?

Wally Worm knew what to do–
Saved the giggle just for you!
When this poem's at its end–
Pass your giggle to a friend!

Hooray! We're Different!

If a moose wore pajamas
would he be the same
as a horse in a hammock
sleeping in the rain

Would a robin in the spring
sing just like a lark
or hoot like an hooty owl
wide awake in thedark

Would a pig with a mustache
Underneath his nose
look like an ostrich
or smell more like a rose

Could a mouse in suspenders
walk very, very far
all the way up to the moon
or the tiptop of a star

When you wear your pajamas
Or suspenders or such
are you the same person
 or not so very much

The truth of the matter
is not so hard to see
You are not like a moose
or even just like me

You're not like a horse
or a pig or a duck
Not like all your friends –
What a grand piece of luck!

Your just like yourself
and like nobody other
not even like your sister
or big older brother

People are just people
They're not all the same
So why do you think
they have different names

Like Ozzie, Sam or Lizzie
or Ziggy, Beth or Mike–
God has made us different
So we're not all alike!

Just look how you look
in your own special way
And cheer for the difference

HIP-HIP-YAY-HOORAY!

Racing Weevil

I had a Weevil I used to race
Just outside London, or some such place
I'd wear my fundles (they're just like spats)
new gray breeches and old slouch hat

I'd bet my pennies; a dozen a race
Ran my Weevil at breakneck pace
Spurred his weblings; jabbed his snout
Till that Weevil was plain run out!

Turn one, he's leading! (By just a touch)
Turn two, he's losing (I feared as much)
Turn three, he's even (I dreamed of fame)
Turn four, disaster! My Weevil's lame!

The race now over, my pennies, lost
My Weevil hobbled, his weblings tossed
So if you've a Weevil you'd like to race
Just outside London, or some such place

Recall my story– of luck run down
Gather your fundles and drive to town
Rush to market, and plop them down

Fundles and breeches and old slouch hat
Spurs and weblings and ratta-tat-tat
Plop them down– To the ground, I say!
Gather your pennies; be on your way!
On your way and escape that place
Learn from me: Weevils just can't race!

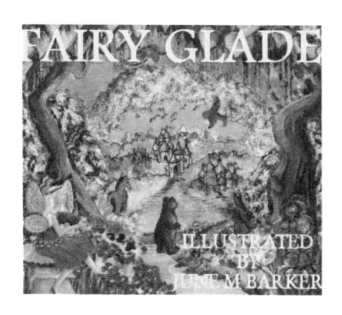

FAIRY GLADE

ILLUSTRATED BY JUNE M BARKER

Gentiana sniffed the fresh breeze
moistened by a recent spring rain.
She stood beneath a fern frond
as roly-poly raindrops
hung momentarily suspended,
before falling earthward
to .splosh. happily in a puddle.

Fairies don.t like rain, you know!
It makes their wings soggy,
sometimes too soggy to fly.
Gentiana didn.t much like soggy wings.

When the rain had come
she had hidden under the fern,
away from the rain drops.

Now that the storm had passed
she started again for Yerba.s house,
deep inside Mistywood Forest

Yerba lived there, inside the forest,
in a cave cut beneath a towering elm.
He was an ancient bear, very old .
too old, in fact, to gather food anymore.

So Gentiana visited Yerba everyday
and brought him sweet honey,
and fresh meadow berries,
and cool water from the brook,
and told stories of .Fairy Glade.

That.s what fairies do, you know .
visit elders and tend their needs,
and keep them comfortable,
until Sherpa comes for them.

Sherpa comes for everyone in the end,
to take them away to somewhere
that only he and fairies know about.

Most animals never worry much
about where Sherpa will take them.
Fairies like Gentiana see to that.

"Good Morning, Yerba!"
Gentiana called in her sing-song way.

"How are you this fine day?"

Yerba did not answer,
but only smiled a little smile
as he lay quietly on the cave floor.

Gentiana knew it was Yerba.s last day.
She had cared for elders
ever since time was an infant,
and she knew Sherpa
would soon call for the old bear.

"Come Yerba, eat some sweet berries,"
Gentiana coaxed him softly,
but Yerba was not hungry.

"Come Yerba, taste this sweet honey."
Her fairy wings fanned his face,
but Yerba did not even lift his head.

"Come Yerba, drink this cool water."
She offered him a cup filled to its brim,
but Yerba sipped only a little bit.

Gentiana fluttered her delicate wings
and hovered over the old bear,
lying tired and worn on the cave floor.

Dipping her hand into a small pouch
hanging loosely from her side
she lovingly smiled at Yerba,
then sprinkled fairy dust on him.

"There," she whispered.
"Now you can rest with smiles."

"Yes," thought Yerba,
"I must rest awhile...."
Then quietly he slipped away.

"Come out here, Yerba!"
Called a voice from the sunlight.

Yerba opened his eyes to see Sherpa
standing tall beside the elm.

He felt again the strength of youth .
when he had run his fastest,
and played happily in the meadow.

He arose and followed Sherpa
out into the bright morning sunlight.

As Gentiana watched him leave
she sang an age old fairy song
from another time and place .

"Ancient creatures gently rest,
by the Sherpa ever blest.
Brightly shining here below,
with their spirits gently go."

Gentiana was most happy now.
Yerba no longer felt the pain of age
because Sherpa would lead him
to the spirit life beyond the woodland,
far away where the land always smiles,
to a glade Gentiana knew was home.

RAYMOND COPP

CINCHONA SYMPHONY

ILLUSTRATED
BY
DARRYL LOREN HOWE

On the Andean mountainside warmed by springtime sunlight, winter snows become rivulets; then brooks and streams.

Philippe Garza, son of Ernesto the tailor, climbed the precipitous slope in search of his burro, Chupe, missing from the valley village.

Strong down slope winds blew cold from the mountaintop as Phillipe hailed his friend, "Chupe! Chupe! Come burro!"

A distant echo lured the boy from one unfamiliar path to another
until the last disappeared into a dark forest of tall Cinchona trees.

Deep within the grove stood an evergreen much taller than the rest.
A Cinchona of profound beauty and elegance, a pillar of majestic bearing
that seemed to draw Philippe to its captivating grandeur.
The Cinchona held its needled branches both upward to heaven
and outward as a mother opens her arms to her lonely child.

Philippe sat under the tree, his back against the strong, aged trunk.
Fallen brown needles on the ground soon wiggling under his feet,
moving like a wave on the ocean, until a small brown-gray mouse
popped his head into the sunlight and looked at the strange visitor,
before squeaking in disgust and submerging once again
to take a circuitous route around the intruder to the nearby meadow.

The "kee-e-e! kee-e-e!" of a Peregrine falcon perched on the tippy-top branch of the Cinchona signaled the never-ending struggle for survival in nature. That piercing call of the winged hunter froze in place a gray-brown rabbit which had sought protection of the giant tree's lower branches.

A mother fox summoned her kittens, "Kip! Kip!"from their hiding spot
in the tall, nearly green grass growing like a fence around the tree's border.

Philippe Garza felt the warmth of the sun on his boyish face and relaxed on a blanket of Cinchona needles while wild flowers blossomed in the meadow. The symphony of nature complimented by the background clamor of wind, rhythmically roaring through the majestic tree's outstretched arms aggravated a pair of Martens trying to build a nest in the swaying branches.

The boy, sensing the presence of another, opened his eyes to behold an angel,
bathed in an eerie warm glow and wearing a white satin gown as in a dream.
Philippe watched unbelieving as the spirit being moved closer.
and touched his hand with the cool wash of divine presence.

She did not speak but seemed to pass through and around his body. He felt a tingling warmth in his stomach as the angel entered his being and an exhilaration as the spirit dove down to his deepest inner self, pausing briefly, almost as if to enjoy again the sensation of being alive.

For just an instant in time, not measurable by any mortal being
the boy and spirit were as one, two souls connected in one body
sharing, in a universal language, knowledge of life and nature.
Then as quickly as the angel had appeared, she vanished into nothingness.

The boy stepped from under the Cinchona's low branches into the sunlight where Chupe stood before him, head bowed eating the sweet spring grass. Philippe called "Come here, Chupe!" and led the burro down to the village.

Philippe often returned to the Cinchona tree in the mountain forest
to experience time and again the beauty of nature and symphony of life.
With each trip the boy, and then the man, summoned the angel forth
to share the freedoms of spirit life with pleasures of the world.

In his final days, Philippe journeyed to the Andean mountain one last time and sat against the strong, aged trunk of the grand Cinchona.

He watched a mouse surface nearby, squeak in disgust and submerge again.

He heard "kee-e-e! kee-e-e!" as the Peregrine announced its hunt for prey.

Playful fox kittens, and the brown rabbit, and the animals of the wood, added their voices to the harmonic sound of the Cinchona symphony.

When Philippe closed his eyes a final time, he dreamed of the angel.
who came to him, more beautiful than before, and took him by the hand.
He beheld a whole host of forest animals, large and small, hunter and hunted
watching in harmony as the spirit led him out into the meadow.

Philippe felt the angel's touch and sensed again their souls fusing together. And as the grand Cinchona watched approvingly overhead, the spirit revealed with a kiss, understanding that only comes from being one with the Creator.

Summer Daydream

My fantasy backyard play land
Its grass is a carpet of dreams
With trees as the statues of warriors
Make real the make believe scene

My sandbox a nobleman's castle
A fortress to wall out the foe
My swings the bowstrings of archers
Flinging needles sent row after row

Our enemy charges the ramparts
Hurls lances and missiles our way
With ladders to climb our strong bastion
Only bravery shall save us the day!

The sky is the blue of our banner
Held high as we stand on the tower
White clouds as our billowy stanchions
Protect us in our finest hour!

Now time for the last desperate battle
For freedom and truth we must die
Only Mother is calling me homeward
For lunch we have blueberry pie!

The Wishing Star

I'll build for us a rocket ship
And land it on a starry strip
Nestled in the Milky Way
Several million miles away

I haven't picked a star for us
Like Scorpios or Sirius
So maybe one that's rather far
Like the magic Wishing Star

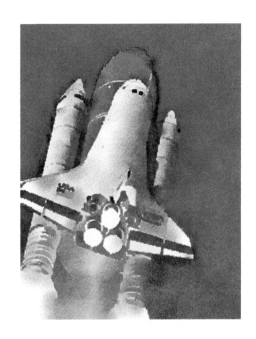

I'd like to take you on the trip
Aboard our cozy rocket ship
To loop around Aquarius
And race against the Pegasus

Our trip should take about a week
So we should pack a lunch to eat
Like celery and mayonnaise
Or maybe eggs with hollandaise

There isn't much to do in space
Once we've left our earthly place
So we would snuggle close as one
To marvel at each passing sun

I'll be your planetary guide
As fiery comets swirl outside
Then whisper cosmic poetry
About our daring rocketry

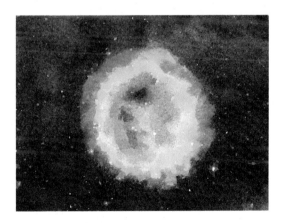

We'll marvel at each Nova's birth
On our journey far from Earth
From the place we left behind
Where our lives became entwined

And when we reach the Wishing Star
We'll settle down right where we are
To treasure each supernal view
As star crossed lovers often do

CPSIA information can be obtained
at www.ICGtesting.com
Printed in the USA
BVOW05s0237050817
491227BV00001B/1/P